Praise for Claire Thompson's *Handyman*

"Claire Thompson has really outdone herself with Handyman...The plotting was smooth and flowed from one scene to the next. The drama between the two was realistic and added that extra bit of flair that made Handyman such a delicious story."

~ *Hayley, Fallen Angel Reviews*

"Handyman is a heart-wrenching tale of personal discovery and growth that I couldn't put down...This book definitely will be placed in my keeper pile to be enjoyed again in the future."

~ *Mystical Nymph, Literary Nymphs Reviews*

"Claire Thompson can write exceptional romance, especially those between men. There are not too many authors who can write gay romance with such emotion and angst as Thompson can. I have read many other titles by this author, and I have to say that HANDYMAN may be her best yet... HANDYMAN is a very special romance between two people whose chemistry is smoking hot as well as having the utmost respect for each other's lifestyles. The journey for Will and Jack's love is a very welcome read, and Claire Thompson deserves the La Grande Mort award for writing a truly incredible story."

~ *Kate Garrabrant, RRTErotic*

Look for these titles by

Claire Thompson

Now Available:

Our Man Friday

Polar Reaction

Handyman

Claire Thompson

A Samhain Publishing, Ltd. publication.

Samhain Publishing, Ltd.
577 Mulberry Street, Suite 1520
Macon, GA 31201
www.samhainpublishing.com

Handyman

Print ISBN: 978-1-60504-319-7
Digital ISBN: 1-60504-180-7

Editing by Sasha Knight
Cover by Angela Waters

First Samhain Publishing, Ltd. electronic publication: September 2008
First Samhain Publishing, Ltd. print publication: July 2009

Dedication

For Tracey and Jean, with endless thanks for their support, wisdom and humor.

Chapter One

Straight.

The word popped into Will's head. Whether or not he was actively thinking about it, he couldn't help but scope out any guy, no matter how old or unattractive.

The man standing on his front porch appeared to be in his mid-forties. He had dark brown hair threaded with gray and deep-set gray-blue eyes above a prominent nose. The words *Affordable Improvements* were stitched in small red letters on his pale blue denim work shirt. He wore dark blue jeans over scuffed brown work boots. His hands were large, the fingers thick and blunt. They looked like the hands of someone who made his living with them.

"Hi. I'm Jack Crawford. You called about doing some renovations to your kitchen?"

"I did. Come in." They shook hands, Jack's grip firm and friendly. For some odd reason Will didn't want to let go. He found himself wondering for a split second if maybe he'd been wrong. Maybe the guy was gay? His cock twitched at the thought. He looked up into the man's face, but saw nothing there but an innocuous, polite smile. Feeling a little foolish, he dropped Jack's hand and gestured for him to follow.

Until three months ago, Will had lived in the city, working as a trader for a prestigious investment bank by day and living it up in the Manhattan club scene by night. Sleep, he used to laughingly tell his friends and lovers, was overrated.

After running all day on too much coffee and the adrenaline rush of playing with big money on Wall Street, Will had increasingly found the need for sleeping pills and booze to unwind. His doctor had warned him if he didn't slow down from his fast-paced, hectic lifestyle, he was going to burn out before thirty-five.

When his boss, barely fifty-five, dropped dead in front of him of a massive heart attack, Will, deeply shaken, had finally stepped back to assess his life. He took a leave of absence from the firm, determined to take stock of his life and figure out what the hell he was doing. He decided to buy a house in the suburbs, settling on an old Tudor he'd snagged for a song.

The quiet, tree-lined Scarsdale neighborhood was quite a change from the frenetic, pressured pace of the city. He missed the clubs and the vibrancy of city nightlife but was determined to give this new life a try, at least for the six-month leave he'd negotiated with his company.

He hadn't counted on the cost and work involved in renovating a hundred-year-old home, the last updates apparently done in the sixties, when avocado green and vomit orange were the preferred color scheme.

He had already had a bad experience with an electrician he'd hired, who had started out gung ho but then faded away, leaving wires dangling and work incomplete until Will had been forced, in absentia, to fire him.

Jack, at least, had been referred by a friend who said he did good, reliable work at a reasonable price and, most importantly, showed up to finish what he started.

"What were you thinking of having done?" Jack looked around the long, narrow kitchen with its peeling linoleum floor, green cabinets and orange countertops.

"What am I not thinking of having done is more the question," Will quipped. "The woman who lived here bought the place with her husband sixty years ago. She told me her kids had been trying to get her to move for the past thirty years since he died."

"Why do you think she finally moved?" Jack seemed genuinely curious, which surprised Will. Usually these workmen types just wanted to get down to business and were happiest when left alone.

"Her bones, she said. Just couldn't handle the cold anymore. She said from November to April she just ached with it. Her daughters finally convinced her to move down south with them. Lucky for me, I guess. It's very hard to find anything even remotely affordable in Westchester County anymore. This place is pretty rundown—I didn't realize quite how much. The basement is a disaster of crumbling concrete and mold. The upstairs bathroom has what must be the original old porcelain tub, complete with rust stains. I had a shower added the first week I was here—I couldn't imagine bathing in that tub.

"The attic is filled with stuff she forgot or didn't feel like taking—things like cracked old rolls of linoleum, stacks of old window frames, mounds of ancient newspapers and magazines and various boxes that probably haven't been opened since World War II.

"I've been here a month and I've barely scratched the surface. I tore down the hideous flocked wallpaper in the front hall and powder room, and I pulled up the ancient carpets, but now the hardwood floors need refinishing and I haven't decided what I want to do with the walls."

As they stood looking at the dismal room, Will said, "She told me she'd recently had the kitchen remodeled, and wasn't it lovely. Apparently, by 'recently' she meant forty years ago." He laughed and Jack smiled in return.

"I figured we could start in here. Get a stove that actually works and cabinets any color but that hideous green. I was thinking stone tile for the floors, but maybe hardwood would be better. What do you think?"

They discussed countertops, cabinets, flooring, light fixtures, colors and possibly breaking down a wall to open the space into the dining room. Jack had pulled a small notebook from his hip pocket, into which he was busily scribbling notes with a small pencil. A swatch of thick hair fell over his forehead, brushing into his eyes as he wrote. He looked like he needed a haircut. Will glanced at his ring finger and saw no telltale golden band. Not that that meant anything—he knew lots of married guys who didn't wear wedding rings.

"I'll work something up for you," Jack said at last, tucking the small notebook into his back pocket. "Gather some prices and bring you some samples. I'll bring a couple of catalogues from the home-improvement warehouses so we can get a feel for what you're looking for.

"I've got a job I need to finish but I should be able to wrap it up by tomorrow. How about I come back day after tomorrow? I'll have a better handle on costs then."

"Sounds like a plan. See you then."

Jack stroked the curve of wood with his fingers, closing his eyes to enjoy the sensual feel of the smooth grain. Emma used to laugh at him when she'd catch him in his workroom, "making love" to the furniture he built. He had to admit, it was a labor of love. He didn't produce much—the occasional chair or table for their home, nothing for actual sale—but each piece somehow became a part of him by the time he was done with it.

His real work, the one-man renovation company he'd started twenty years before, had provided a decent income for his family. They'd bought a three-bedroom house in the north end of New Rochelle before prices went through the roof. The mortgage was paid off. The boys had grown up and moved out. And Emma was dead.

He leaned his cheek against the wood, the word echoing in his mind. *Dead.* She woke up one morning with a terrible headache and said she felt sick to her stomach. He'd brought her tea, assuming she was getting the flu. She drank a few sips, set it down and turned very pale.

"Jack," she said, her voice urgent. And then...she was gone. The autopsy revealed a ruptured brain aneurysm. At the age of forty-two his wife of twenty-four years was gone. Just like that.

Though two years had passed, he still sometimes woke up in the middle of the night, reaching for her. Recently a few friends had begun rumblings about trying to fix him up with someone new. Though he knew they meant well, he wasn't interested.

He'd grown up with Emma. They knew each other so well he sometimes felt as if she were more of a sister than a lover and wife. They were best friends, no question of that. But now that he'd had time to mourn her loss, he knew theirs had not been a passionate union.

Not for the first time he wondered if they would have married at all if she hadn't gotten pregnant. He'd had plans back then to go to college in the city with his best buddy, Luke, while she was planning to attend a local nursing school. Odds are they would have drifted apart, met new people, gone their separate ways.

How different his life might have been, without the challenge of an instant family at such a young age. He would have gone to college, maybe traveled the world. He might have become a teacher or an engineer. *He* might have been the one hiring a handyman to come into his fancy Scarsdale home.

Jack shook his head as if to clear it. These kinds of thoughts were never fruitful. What was the point of wondering at what might have been? He'd done the right thing by Emma and they had two wonderful sons and a good life.

You play the hand you're dealt, he said firmly to himself.

Two days later found Jack on Will's doorstep, catalogues and a toolbox in his hand. He'd called the evening before, pleased when Will suggested he come by early. Glancing at his watch, he hoped it wasn't *too* early.

As he waited for Will to answer the door he looked around the front yard. It was a small yard by neighborhood standards, but already daffodils and tulips were popping up in brilliant yellows, reds and purples in the flowerbeds in front of the house and along the old stone walkway leading to the door. The beds needed weeding and the lawn needed mowing. He made a mental note to recommend a gardener for the rich city boy.

It being a Wednesday, Jack wondered what Will did that allowed him to be home during the week. Not that he'd ask. Jack knew better than to pry into the lives of the people he did work for. He'd learned as friendly as they might seem, they were generally just being polite. He was polite back, but that was as far as it went.

Though it was only eight o'clock, Jack had been up for hours. Since Emma had died he could never sleep much past the sun's rising, though that didn't stop him from lying awake long into the night, his mind refusing to shut off even though he didn't have a whole hell of a lot to think about.

For the first few months after she'd died, he started to use alcohol as a way to calm himself down enough for sleep. It began innocently enough, he supposed—with a shot or two of bourbon to unwind while he read or watched TV. After a while he was drinking more than a shot or two—sometimes drinking half a bottle before he'd drugged himself enough to pass out.

Each day he'd take mental stock—did he have enough liquor to get through the night? He would wake up, the bottle beckoning beside the bed like an old friend. Why not take a sip or two to start the day? To get him through?

One morning after an especially horrific nightmare in which he watched Emma and the boys plummet to their deaths while he stood helplessly by, he bypassed the tiny shot glass, instead grabbing the glass he normally used for water. With shaking hands he poured several ounces and drank them in a gulp. Closing his eyes, he sighed with relief as the burn in his gut shifted to a welcome heaviness in his head, blotting out the bloody, broken images from his dreams.

He lay back on the bed and passed into a woozy doze. When he came awake with a start several hours later, his first glance was again toward the bottle. Only opened the night before, it lay empty on its side.

Deeply shaken, he called his baby sister, Anna, who lived twenty miles away and was a stay-at-home mother.

"Anna. I need help. I'm becoming a drunk."

While he was waiting for her to arrive he cleared out his liquor cabinet, opening and pouring out the contents of each bottle into the kitchen sink.

Anna arrived armed with coffee and donuts. Though she

was a full ten years younger than he, he'd always felt closest to her of his three sisters.

They spent the morning at his kitchen table, a fine old piece he'd built himself from a huge slab of oak someone had been looking to get rid of when they were finishing out their basement.

She calmed his fears about becoming an alcoholic, as she herself was a recovering one. "You realized you were drinking too much and so you did what?"

"I called you."

"That's not all you did. You got rid of your stash. You recognized drinking half a bottle of whiskey at seven a.m. wasn't a wise thing to do. I don't mean to minimize the experience, but I don't think labeling yourself a drunk is terribly useful right now. If you were an alcoholic, trust me, it would take you way more than one drink in the morning to admit you had a problem, much less do anything about it."

Anna convinced him to see a therapist, just for a while, to work through some of his feelings of loss and move on with his life. He'd gone, mainly to please her, but it hadn't really helped all that much.

Time—that great healer—had done the most, along with getting himself back to work and keeping busy. He still missed Emma, but not with the sudden, shocking wrench of pain he experienced during those first few months when he'd realize anew he would never see her again.

The front door opened. Will was dressed in blue jeans, his white shirt unbuttoned over a smooth, tan chest. He was drying his hair with a towel, his face ruddy from a recent shower.

"Hey, sorry. I didn't hear the bell at first. Please come in. I overslept."

The scent of shampoo and soap assailed Jack as he

brushed by Will to head toward the kitchen. Will followed. "Want some coffee? I just put some on. I haven't had breakfast yet. Would you like something? I have some croissants coming out of the oven in a minute."

Jack started to refuse out of habit, but the coffee smelled wonderful and the small cup he'd had two hours before was but a distant memory. "Coffee would be fine, if it's not too much trouble."

Will took two mugs from the cabinet beside the sink. The wood looked to be of high quality, but it had been painted a seasick green color, which clashed violently with the pale orange countertops.

Will placed the mugs and the pot of coffee on the counter, along with a small carton of half and half and a bowl of sugar. "Help yourself," he said with a smile, as he poured himself a cup.

As Jack did so, Will took the rolls out of the oven, filling the room with the yeasty, buttery aroma of fresh-baked croissants. Jack realized he was hungry. Will put the steaming hot rolls on the counter and moved to the refrigerator and retrieved the butter.

Returning to the counter, he sat at one of the two barstools there and pointed to the other. "Have a seat. We can go over what you've brought while we eat."

Will pulled apart a roll and smeared it with butter, which instantly melted into a pooled yellow glaze. Jack's mouth watered.

"Go on," Will urged. "Have one. I can't possibly eat all these."

Jack took one and bit into the savory crust. "Thanks. I didn't even know I was hungry until I smelled them."

They drank coffee and looked through the catalogues, notes

and blueprints on which Jack had drawn up a few ideas for the kitchen. Will seemed entirely uninterested in the cost of the project, focused exclusively on what he liked.

Jack was used to working with people in affluent neighborhoods like this one, people who had money to burn, but they weren't usually as young as Will seemed to be. On an impulse, Jack said, "If you don't mind my asking, how old are you?"

A smile curved Will's mouth. Jack immediately regretted the question. He'd broken his cardinal rule of not prying into clients' personal lives, no matter how innocuous the question.

"I'm thirty. Just celebrated the big three-o two weeks ago. Why do you ask?"

"Oh, uh, no reason really." Jack felt the heat rise in his face and cursed himself. What the hell was he blushing about? What did he care what this kid thought of him? "I have two sons," he threw out. "One nearly as old as you."

"What? No way. You don't look old enough to have grown sons."

"Well, thanks, I guess. I'm forty-four. My oldest is twenty-five. His little brother is twenty-three."

He watched Will do the math in his head. "Why, that means you had your first child when you were nineteen."

Jack nodded. "Yep. Married my high school sweetheart."

"Shotgun wedding," Will said with a grin. Then, "I'm sorry. I didn't mean—"

"No, it's okay." Jack laughed. "It's actually true. It's amazing how one night can change the direction of your life."

Will nodded slowly, and for some reason Jack noticed his eyes were green.

✧

To keep himself sharp and his investment portfolio up to date, Will had taken up day trading out of his home. Using advanced analytical software, his connections in the financial markets and his direct line to the trading desk at his bank, Will continued to make a very nice living without the daily pressures of life on Wall Street.

The phone rang. Will let it ring a moment while he executed a trade. Satisfied, he glanced at the phone and saw it was the office.

"Spencer," he said brusquely.

"Will. It's Guy. Trenton's going to be here today, in the flesh. Power lunch. Chosen few. I think I can finagle you a spot at his table if you get your ass down here. Lunch is at one. You in?"

Joseph Trenton was the CEO of Will's firm, which had offices all over the country and around the world. Trenton liked to hold what were known as power lunches but which were really little more than popularity contests, so it seemed to Will. He'd been invited once or twice, permitted to sit near the boss and bask in his regal glow. He'd been largely ignored, except when Trenton turned to him at one point and asked his name.

"William Spencer, Mr. Trenton."

Jovially the large, beefy man had boomed, "Call me Joey."

Guy Gray, a trading buddy at work, lived for these lunches, believing they were the key to opening doors to more power and prestige within the organization.

Be that as it may, sitting in his jeans and bare feet in his comfortable den, Will found it hard to muster the enthusiasm Guy obviously expected of him.

Not to mention, he was expecting Jack at ten.

Today Jack was going to begin the gutting process, ripping out the old cabinets and, if he had time, knocking down the wall that separated the kitchen from the dining room. He'd warned Will the kitchen would be pretty much unusable for a while.

Will had spent the morning clearing out the cabinets, mildly surprised to find how much he'd already managed to fill them in the few months he'd been in the new house. Stacks of dishes and rows of glasses and cups covered his dining room table, along with boxes of spices and canned goods.

"Sorry, Guy. Can't make it. But thanks for thinking of me."

"Okay, if you're sure. I should warn you, though."

Here it comes, Will thought with a wry grin at the phone. Guy loved to preface gossip with that phrase, especially negative gossip about the person involved. Will had learned for the most part to ignore whatever followed.

Guy lowered his voice conspiratorially. "Talk among the secretaries is that your office is going to be given to Jenkins. His numbers were through the roof last month and the big guys want to reward him. I know they promised to save your spot, but, buddy, you might want to rethink this sabbatical thing. You may have left with the title of golden boy, but you could end up coming back to a broom closet for an office."

Will laughed, surprised to find he really didn't care. "I'll take my chances. Give my regards to Joey."

Will stood at the doorway of the kitchen watching Jack work. He was on a ladder, dismantling a row of cabinets. Will suppressed a sudden fantasy of moving behind him and sliding his hands beneath the loose work shirt to feel the supple movement of Jack's back muscles as he worked.

When Jack had arrived that morning he'd refused Will's offer of coffee and muffins, which oddly disappointed Will, though of course he hadn't pressed. Jack was, after all, just a hired hand.

Jack carefully lowered a cabinet to the ground. "We'll want to order a dumpster," Jack said, startling him. He hadn't realized Jack was aware of his presence. "I have the name of a good local company, if you want me to set it up."

"Sure. That would be fine. Whatever you think."

Jack nodded and turned back to his work. After a few minutes he reached into his back pocket and pulled out a balled-up bandana he drew across his forehead.

Though it wasn't quite April, spring had definitely arrived and the room was a little warm, especially if one was exerting as Jack was. "Let me open some windows," Will offered, stepping into the room.

"Careful. There're nails and debris on the floor. It might be better if you just stayed out of here while I do this. At least until I can get the mess cleaned up."

"Oh. Well, okay. Feel free to open windows. There's a screen on the back door so you can open that too. I'll just be in my den working. Uh, thanks."

"No problem," Jack said, though he was apparently too intent on unscrewing a difficult bolt from the wall to turn around.

Will went back to his den and sat in front of his computer, but instead of returning to his work he stared out the window, distracted. What the hell was wrong with him? Why had he made muffins for the handyman, for crying out loud? What did he care if the man was sweating?

It wasn't like he was potential play material. He was straight. He was married, for God's sake. He had grown kids nearly Will's age. He wasn't particularly good-looking, though Will couldn't deny there was a certain appealing strength in his features, and his body was definitely nothing to sneer at.

He had the heavy, thick muscles of a man who used his body to earn his living. Will looked down at himself, mentally comparing. His was a strong body as well, but by design. He worked out religiously three days a week at the gym, and played tennis and golf. He kept a set of barbells in his bedroom, using them while he watched TV to keep his muscles strong.

What it would be like to earn a living by the sweat of one's brow? Raised in the city by wealthy professionals, Will had been groomed practically from birth to attend Columbia University, where he'd obtained both his undergraduate degree and MBA.

He wondered if Jack ever cracked a book. *That's unfair*, he admonished himself. *You know nothing about the guy. For all you know, he's got the IQ of Einstein. Even if he doesn't, so what? Stop judging someone by what they do instead of who they are.*

Why was he judging at all? It wasn't as if he were interested in the guy as a potential lover. He rubbed at his cock through his pants as Jack's image floated unannounced and uninvited into his mind.

Annoyed with himself, he reached for the phone. He'd call Paul and ask him out. Paul, with his dark, sensual good looks and insatiable sexual appetite, would distract him from whatever the hell it was he needed distracting from.

Chapter Two

"Man, you weren't kidding. This place looks like a bomb hit it. What's with all the dust?" Paul said as they entered the house. They'd only stopped by Will's place so he could pick up an overnight bag before heading to Paul's for the night.

"Yeah. Jack says that's because the wall he's tearing down is plaster. They used plaster in these older houses, before drywall was invented. He made me put on a dust mask when I came into the kitchen to watch him."

"You came in to watch the guy work? What for? Afraid he's going to steal the silverware?"

Will felt himself flush and he jerked his head in dissent. "No, nothing like that. I'm just kind of...interested. In the process, I mean. I never owned a house before. It's exciting to be in at the beginning of the renovations. Jack and I are going to create the perfect kitchen, designed especially for me. He has so many good ideas. He drew up blueprints and everything."

Paul tilted his head inquiringly at Will. "Do I have something to be jealous about here? Is that what you're trying to tell me?"

"What?" Will burst out laughing, aware he was nearly guffawing, which made him even more self-conscious. "No. No, no, no." He shook his head for emphasis. "The guy is some old married dude. Jesus, Paul. You think everyone is up for grabs, as long as they have a dick."

"And your point is...?" Paul raised his eyebrows in mock question.

"God, shut up." Will headed toward his study. "I just need to check something on my computer and I'll be ready to go."

Later that night Will knelt behind Paul, his cock poised to enter his lover's tight ass. He stroked himself in preparation as Paul wiggled provocatively toward him. He closed his eyes and pressed against the entrance, drawing a moan from Paul. The hot grip of muscle felt so good as he slid himself deep inside.

What would it be like to fuck Jack or to be fucked by him? He'd played down his interest to Paul, but in fact his fantasies skated along a hot, dangerous path he knew would only lead to frustration. He could pretend to Paul and to himself he wasn't interested, but he was—he definitely was.

All thought flew from his head as he began to rock and thrust. Paul held himself up with one hand, using the other to massage his own shaft in time to Will's motion.

"Yeah, baby. Yeah." Paul arched back to take Will deeper. Will gripped Paul's hips as his body coiled for release. He grunted his pleasure, thrusting in a series of hard spasms as he ejaculated.

His heart thumping, he sagged against Paul as Paul finished himself off with his hand and fell forward, taking Will with him. They lay together, their ragged breathing slowing in tandem as they recovered.

"Don't get too comfy," Paul announced with a grin. "I'm going to do you next, baby."

Will awoke to the sound of his cell phone ringing and vibrating in his pants pocket. His pants were in a heap on the floor near the bed. Heavy curtains at the windows shut out the light. Will stumbled toward his pants and fumbled for the phone. By the time he got to it, he'd missed the call.

He glanced at the digital clock beside the still-sleeping Paul. Eight-fifteen. Eight-fifteen! He'd told Jack he could come back at eight. *Shit.* Why had he stayed over at Paul's place? Usually he liked to hightail it out of there once he'd gotten what he'd come for. And he hadn't meant to sleep this late, damn it.

After a lengthy session in bed, he'd let Paul convince him to soak in the hot tub he kept on his deck. They'd shared champagne, finishing the bottle between them before returning to the bed for more leisurely fucking until they drifted into an alcohol and sex-induced coma.

Stepping into the bathroom for privacy, he called back the missed number. Jack's deep, gravelly voice answered. "Affordable Improvements."

"Jack, it's Will. Will Spencer. Look, I'm really sorry. You're probably there waiting and I—"

"What?" There was a pause and then Jack continued, "No. No, I'm not at your place, if that's what you mean. That's why I was calling. I'm running late. A neighbor had a little emergency with their plumbing. I just wanted to let you know. I should be there by about nine or nine-thirty. I need to pick up a few things. The dumpster should be delivered late this morning too."

"Oh. Okay. No problem. I'll see you when you get there. Uh, here. When you get to my place, that is."

Feeling like a fool on a number of levels, Will hung up the phone.

"Hey, who're you talking to?" Paul's sleepy voice reached him.

"Um, nobody."

"Good, then get back in here and service me, stud."

Will opened the door and again the scent of shampoo and soap wafted from him. His wavy light brown hair was wet, a towel still in his hand. *This guy showers a lot*, Jack thought with amusement.

"Hi. Sorry about the mix up earlier." Will stepped back and waved Jack in. "I—I was actually out when you called. I got us some bagels and coffee. I thought we could sit in the living room and go over the catalogues one more time. I'm having some second thoughts about the cabinet styles we talked about."

Jack nodded without comment. He hoped he'd be able to convince Will to stick with what he'd selected, since they'd already placed the order at the home-improvement warehouse. He followed the younger man into the living room and sat across from him at a card table where Will had placed the blueprints and design notes.

He noted the two cups of coffee and the bagels set on a plate and smiled. Will really was a very nice guy. All too often, especially in neighborhoods like this one, Jack was treated like the hired help he was, sometimes instructed to use only the back entrance, and to speak only with the maid if he needed something. Not that he particularly minded—he came to do a job and he didn't care what door he used to get there.

Will began to talk about the cabinets, pointing and gesturing at the various styles in the catalogue. Slowly and calmly Jack talked him down, relieved when Will finally agreed what they'd ordered was the best fit for the kitchen.

Will passed the plate of bagels toward Jack. "They were still warm when I bought them. I hope you like bagels. I could toast one if you want."

"No, this is fine. Thanks very much. It's very nice of you to keep feeding me like this." Jack reached for a bagel and spread some cream cheese on it. He was mildly amused to see Will watching him anxiously, as if he'd baked the bread himself and was waiting for Jack's approval.

Jack ate the bagel quickly and slurped some of the coffee, though by now he'd already had three cups before this one. "I've got some stuff out in the truck. I'll just get to work."

"Wait."

Jack looked at him expectantly, trying to hide his minor irritation, as he was eager to get on with it. Will stared at him, his face working, and Jack had the impression he was trying to come up with something to say. "We were going to talk about the handles. The handles and knobs for the cabinet doors and the drawers."

Jack stood. "Plenty of time for that. The cabinets won't even be delivered for a week. I'll pick up some samples and we'll be able to make a more informed decision then. Okay?"

"Yeah. Yeah, sure. I'll be in my den working, if you need me."

Because he had been curious, Jack took the opportunity from this segue. "What is it you do, anyway, if you don't mind my asking?"

"I'm a trader. A day trader. At least that's what I'm doing now. I work for an investment bank in the city. Right now I'm on leave. A sabbatical you might say. I was burning out—the pace can be very intense and the stakes are so high—it can about kill you. It did kill my boss."

"No kidding."

"Yeah. He dropped dead of a massive coronary right in the

middle of screaming at a subordinate for making a serious error on a trade. It could just as easily have been me who had cost the firm several million dollars. I think that's what really made it hit home. I realized I was badly in need of some downtime. I decided to take a break and figure out what the hell I want out of the rest of my life."

"A worthy goal," Jack said, nodding. "What does a day trader do exactly?"

"Well, simply put, a day trader is a stock trader who holds positions for a very short time, never keeping positions overnight. They utilize high amounts of leverage and short-term trading strategies to capitalize on small price movements in highly liquid stocks or currencies. There are several different strategies you can use including swing trading and arbitrage. It's a risky business if you don't know what you're doing." He laughed. "Even if you do. But I love it."

Though Jack had almost no idea what Will was talking about, he couldn't help but smile at Will's obvious enthusiasm. His whole face became animated when he spoke about his passion. He reminded Jack of someone, though for the life of him he couldn't think who at just that moment.

"I could show you a few trades on my computer if you want."

Will must be lonely, no matter what he said about needing "downtime". Still, it wasn't his job to provide company—he had been hired to work.

"No, no. That's okay. I'm really behind today. I have another job I have to stop by later this afternoon. I was hoping to get the rest of the wall pulled down and the debris out to the dumpster before I go."

Will nodded, the smile on his face falsely bright. "Of course. You get to work. Let me know if you need anything."

✧

"Would you look at that." Jack, perched on a ladder in the middle of the decimated kitchen, had just removed several of the old drop-ceiling tiles to see what lay beneath.

"What is it?" Will, who had been standing in the doorway of the kitchen watching Jack work, looked up with interest. Was there hidden treasure? Or, more likely, a mouse nest?

Jack pulled out several old panels, yellowed with age, and handed them down to Will. "It's the original old tin ceiling. Looks like the genuine article. I can't believe they'd cover this with ceiling panels."

Grinning down at Will, Jack added, "These tin ceilings were popular in the second half of the nineteenth century and the early twentieth. They were an affordable alternative to the expensive sculpted plaster that was used in the finer homes. This would cost a fortune today."

He pulled a few more panels out of the thin metal framing that held them in place. Will took them and placed them on the growing pile in the middle of the gutted kitchen. The dumpster was already filled with the rest of the debris from the kitchen demolition.

Will moved closer, looking up for inspection. The ceiling hidden beneath consisted of white tin-plated steel pressed into an embossed design that made a pleasing pattern. "That's really cool." He liked the look of the old-fashioned ceiling, but even more, he liked how animated Jack seemed to be over its discovery. In the few days Jack had been coming to work on his kitchen, he mostly kept to himself. He was polite and cordial when they spoke, but nothing more.

Not that Will had the right to expect anything more. Not

that Will *wanted* anything more. Yet he couldn't deny a certain attraction. Something about Jack seemed to grab his attention and hold it.

It was odd, because he wasn't usually attracted to older guys. In fact, most of the guys he dated were younger than he was. Paul, for example, had just turned twenty-five. Not that he and Paul were particularly dating—they were more casual-sex partners, which suited them both. Paul was fun and hot but there was no deep, abiding emotional connection between them.

Will actually prided himself on avoiding guys who seemed to offer the potential messiness of an all-out love affair. Living footloose and fancy-free had suited Will for most of his adult life. It went along with the fast-paced, high-stakes nature of his work.

It was only recently, with his near crash and burn at work, that he'd begun to take stock of his life and his priorities. It hit him maybe something was missing. Something vital.

Surely he wasn't looking toward the handyman in his search for meaning, or whatever the hell it was he was searching for. And yet...and yet he couldn't seem to get the guy out of his mind. He couldn't seem to help hovering nearby when Jack was working—making up excuses to come into the kitchen, thinking up questions that no doubt irritated Jack while he was trying to work.

When Jack was around he couldn't concentrate on his work, and the problem, instead of getting better, was getting worse.

It wasn't that the guy was handsome. His eyes were a little too deep-set beneath heavy brows, giving him a brooding expression. His nose, obviously broken at least once, was large and crooked, the lips beneath perhaps too wide for his face. His beard was heavy, five-o'clock shadow already in evidence by the end of the workday. Though he wasn't especially tall, he was strong and thickly built—giving the impression of power and girth.

In other words, he was most decidedly not Will's typical choice in a man. Will's tastes tended more toward men like Paul—slender, even slight, with the graceful features of a Greek statue. With these men, he realized with a sudden flash of not-really-welcome insight, he was superior—older, wiser, stronger.

With Jack he felt like a kid. Jack didn't seem impressed by the obvious wealth he'd amassed at such an early age or his fancy investment banking job and the degrees that went along with it. He was politely interested when Will talked about his life, but fairly closed off about himself.

Not that Will expected anything different. Just the same, he found himself wondering... Jack challenged something in him. It wasn't that he wanted or expected to get the guy in bed and turn him gay with one well-placed kiss. He just wanted to know more about him.

Why not just take the leap and ask? The last few days Jack had been working, he would take a break by going to his truck and eating a lunch no doubt packed by a dutiful wife. He would either sit in the cab or lean against it, enjoying the fresh spring air. Perhaps today Will would join him.

An hour later Jack popped his head into Will's study, knocking lightly on the doorframe. "Excuse me, just wanted to let you know I'm taking a break. I'm nearly done for today. I piled the boxes of flooring in the kitchen. I'll start to lay it down tomorrow. I think we should return the ceiling panels we bought to replace the old ones and work on restoring that amazing tin ceiling."

"I agree, absolutely." Will swiveled in his desk chair to face Jack. "You know," he said, as if it had just occurred to him. "I have a table and chairs out back on the deck. I was thinking of eating my lunch out there today. Maybe you'd care to join me."

"Oh, I wouldn't want to impose—"

"Not at all. I'd love the company." Will felt his cheeks flush, aware he sounded overeager. He shrugged with an exaggerated casualness. "You know, only if you want to. No big deal."

Jack gave a half-smile and nodded. "Sure. That would be fine. I'll just grab my lunch out of the truck and meet you around back."

Will rushed into the kitchen, sidestepping the pallet laden with boxes of the laminate oak flooring he'd picked from the catalogue and Jack had purchased. He stopped a moment, taking in the empty room, which looked much larger now that the dividing wall between the kitchen and dining room had been pulled down. The higher ceiling would only add to the new feeling of space.

He closed his eyes, trying to imagine this hull of a room turning into the beautiful design Jack had come up with for him. Will was spending a pretty penny. He'd known he wanted something elegant but functional. It remained to be seen if Jack could pull it off.

Remembering his mission, Will tried to think of what to have for lunch. He usually ate out, if he ate a midday meal at all, which wasn't often. Staring into the nearly empty refrigerator, he decided on some cheeses that didn't look too bad, an apple and two bottles of Coke.

Stepping carefully over some nails still left on the floor, he entered the dining room, where the table and sideboard were piled high with the contents of the old kitchen cabinets and drawers. Rummaging a bit, he found a box of crackers. He secured a tray and placed the cheese and crackers on it, along with a plate, a knife and a bottle opener.

When he went out to the deck Jack was already seated at the patio table, a large paper sack in front of him. Will sat across from him, setting down his tray and the bottles of soda. "I brought you a Coke if you'd like it."

"Well, look at that." Jack lifted one of the small green-tinted glass bottles. "I haven't seen a bottle like this in a long time."

"I prefer cola from a glass bottle." Will realized he must sound pompous.

"Me too, I guess. I lived on this stuff back when I was a kid. We'd collect the bottles in a wooden crate with slots for each bottle. We'd take them in for the nickels." He cradled the bottle for a moment, staring down at it. It looked especially small in his large, beefy grasp.

He held out the bottle for further examination. "I got out of the habit of drinking soda years ago. My wife said it was bad for the boys' teeth so we switched to sugar-free Kool-Aid for them, water and seltzer for me."

Will handed the bottle opener to Jack, trying to picture the wife and children in his life. As Jack took it their fingers touched and Will felt an electric current of desire flow between them. He glanced sharply at Jack, who was focused entirely on the bottle. Whatever current had been flowing, it was definitely on a one-way path.

Still, Jack was opening up more than he usually did, perhaps because they were sharing a meal. Jack uncapped the bottle and took a long swig of the cola. With a satisfied sigh, he offered, "That's good. Nice and cold."

"I've got plenty more in the refrigerator." In fact there were only two. He made a mental note to buy more. He watched as Jack unrolled the top of his paper bag and pulled out a large sandwich wrapped in foil.

"Must be nice to have a wife to make you lunch every day."

Will was reminded of the lunches his mother used to pack for him when he was in elementary school.

"Oh." Jack's face crumpled as though he'd received a blow. "I'm a widower. My wife died two years ago."

Without realizing what he was doing, Will reached out a sympathetic hand, touching Jack's bare forearm. Jack looked down at his hand and Will snatched it away. "I—I'm so sorry, Jack. I just assumed—I mean, you're still so young, to lose your wife..."

"Yeah. It was sudden. An aneurysm. Apparently it ruptured in her brain. Five minutes later she was dead."

"Oh my God, that's awful. Were you there when it happened?" The words slipped out before he could censor himself.

"Yeah. She woke up with a really bad headache. I thought she was getting a cold. I went down and made her tea. She took one sip and—" Jack's voice cracked.

"I'm sorry. Please, you don't need to talk about it. It must still be very painful to recall."

"Thanks. I miss her. We were married a long time. We grew up together really. It's kind of a miracle we even stayed together, given we were so young when we tied the knot. Both our parents figured we'd divorce. Maybe we stayed together just to spite them."

Will was startled by this admission, if that's what it was.

Jack grinned at him. "We're creatures of habit. We get used to a thing and then don't think about it much. Babies come, and responsibilities, and we put one foot in front of the other and do what we have to do. We make decisions, or fail to make them, and then we have to live by that. I'm not saying it's right or it's wrong, just human nature."

He shook his head and unwrapped his sandwich, lifting it for a bite. Will was silent, pondering what the hell Jack had meant by his speech, easily the longest one he'd given of a personal nature in the few days of their acquaintance. Was Jack saying he hadn't really been happy in his marriage, but had stayed in it out of habit? Out of duty? Will found himself wildly curious, but didn't dare ask. They weren't friends, after all.

Jack swallowed and gestured toward the food on the tray. "Aren't you going to eat?"

Will, who had completely forgotten about the cheese and crackers, gave a small laugh. "Sure I am. Would you like some cheese and crackers? A slice of apple?"

"What kind of cheeses are those?"

"This one's a Brie. It's an especially good one I get from a gourmet shop in the city. It's got a rich, mushroomy flavor and a silky interior texture. This one is goat cheese. It has a strong flavor and goes very well on these black pepper biscuits."

He noticed Jack was watching him with a small, amused half-smile. Embarrassed, Will added, "I must sound like a pompous ass. I don't mean to. I just love fine cheeses."

"No, no. I'm interested, really. I don't know much about cheese, except for Swiss, Cheddar and American, but I'm up for new things. I find I've become more adventurous as I grow older, rather than less so. Emma's passing made me realize just how short life is. We have to seize every moment and not be afraid to experience something new—even goat cheese."

Will laughed and stuck his hand into the box of imported crackers. He smeared some of the soft, pungent cheese over the cracker and held it out. Jack took it and popped it into his mouth. He raised his eyebrows as he chewed, nodding.

"It's delicious," he pronounced. "I do believe I'll take

another."

Will was ridiculously pleased. He prepared another cracker and Jack again popped it into his mouth. He lifted his bottle of Coke and tilted back his head as he drank. Will had a sudden, almost uncontrollable desire to lean forward and lick along the curve of his throat.

He willed the erection rising in his pants to subside. This was insane. He had a crush on someone as straight as an arrow. What an idiot he was.

The heart wants what it wants. Ruefully, he grinned inwardly, recalling Woody Allen's infamous line about falling in love with his girlfriend's adopted daughter. Stranger partners had come together, he thought, foolishly nursing a tiny bud of hope that sprang out of nowhere in his heart.

He saw Jack was again watching him, that curious half-smile on his face. Will held his gaze, wondering if there was the slightest spark he could cup with his hands and shield while it grew, willing it to blaze into a fire of passion between them. For a long moment they stared into one another's eyes. Will was captivated, though he knew he should turn away.

Jack was the first to break contact. He reached into the paper bag and pulled out a plastic baggie of homemade oatmeal raisin cookies. "Want one?" he said, dispelling the strange erotic mood that had settled over Will. "I made them myself."

Chapter Three

Jack sat staring at the TV. Or rather the TV was on and he was sitting in his favorite recliner, a can of seltzer beside him, an open paperback on his lap, his body facing the screen. But his mind was far away, drifting for some reason back to senior year in high school, before one night's indiscretion turned his world upside down.

Before that year Jack and Luke had been nearly inseparable. Friends since seventh grade, they spent every possible weekend at one or the other's house. They tried out for the same sports teams and studied together for tests. They stayed up late into the night talking and trying to teach each other to play guitar, which neither of them did very well, but both enjoyed.

Though they didn't necessarily share any deep, dark secrets, there was an easy understanding between them. Jack always knew he could count on Luke to watch his back and be there when he needed him. They even talked about going into business together someday, though neither had much idea what they wanted to do.

Then the girls entered the picture. Like Jack and Luke, Emma and Patty were the best of friends. Emma admitted several years into their marriage that she and Patty had discussed and dissected the boys, deciding which one would better suit which girl. He'd been startled by her casual admission they'd ended up tossing a coin.

He thought about the two girls as they had been then—Emma, tall with dark wavy hair and deep brown eyes, her breasts small and high, her hips narrow, and Patty, petite and curvaceous, with strawberry blonde hair and eyes the color of cornflowers. Would he have fallen in love with Patty as easily as he had Emma if she had chosen him instead of Luke?

He could admit now, during the early years of their marriage, he hadn't been in love with Emma. Over the years he'd come to love her and the life they shared. Back then, however, he didn't know what love was.

A shy, gawky teenager, he hadn't dated much when Emma set her sights on him. Emma, outgoing and popular, had floored him when she'd asked him to the autumn dance as her date. Patty had asked Luke, who was less shy than Jack and certainly more experienced.

Luke had already gone all the way with Cindy Stafford. Apparently most of the boys of the senior class had gotten lucky with Cindy at one time or another, but not Jack. Not that he would have refused if she'd shown up naked beneath a raincoat on his doorstep, as she'd purportedly done for the captain of the football team.

Luke had been pretty excited about losing his virginity, though he acknowledged he felt little for Cindy beyond a certain awe at her feminine charms. He admitted he felt kind of sorry for her because of her reputation as a slut, but it hadn't stopped him from leaping at the chance to fuck her.

After the dance, Emma and Jack began dating, "going steady" as they used to say. Emma was an attentive girlfriend, sweet and devoted to Jack. Patty and Luke also became an item. Jack enjoyed being part of a couple for the most part—he was suddenly in the in crowd at school and the source of envy to the boys still not lucky enough to have found a girlfriend.

Though Luke and he remained good friends, something had changed between them. Luke and Patty were sexually active pretty much from the start of their relationship, while Jack and Emma had held back, neither ready to take such a big step. Luke spent every spare moment with Patty, leaving Jack lonely for his friend and for the simple, close times they used to share.

He knew this was part of growing up and tried to accept things as they were. Emma seemed very happy with him, often telling him she loved him and he was the best thing to ever happen to her. Sometimes, though he hadn't been able to articulate it clearly back then, he felt almost suffocated by her constant attentions, but he didn't have the heart, or perhaps the courage, to let her know.

She and Patty remained as close as ever, so it seemed to Jack, who sometimes accidentally overheard his girlfriend on the phone, telling Patty intimate details about their relationship he would never have dreamed of sharing with Luke, no matter how close they were.

Senior year hurtled to a close, drawing Jack along in its wake. Though he was fond of Emma, he was secretly looking forward to leaving her behind once he went off to college with his old friend, Luke.

There had been rumors circulating through the school that Luke and Patty were planning to marry after high school. Luke had bought Patty a friendship ring with a tiny diamond at its center. She'd told anyone who would listen it was an engagement ring. Privately Luke told Jack he had no intention of marrying Patty, but he let her have her little fantasy.

Then, a week before the prom, to the astonishment of those who knew them, Luke and Patty broke up. It happened when

Luke, who was supposed to be away at a sporting event, returned home before schedule. Thinking he'd surprise his girlfriend, he showed up unannounced at her house.

A constant fixture there, he'd knocked on the front door and then let himself in. Patty's parents weren't home but she was. So was Dominic Connor, senior class president, voted most likely to succeed by his classmates. They were nearly naked, thrashing together on the living room couch. Luke took one look and that was that. It was over.

Despite her entreaties to forgive her, he was resolute. Jack had felt both admiration and frustration with Luke. If he really loved her, surely he'd forgive her? It was one stupid mistake, so she'd tearfully assured him. She'd tried to involve Jack, calling him to knock some sense into his friend. "We were studying for the math final. He brought some beer. One thing just led to another. I know it was stupid. I love Luke! We're going to be married! He can't just dump me, can he?"

Apparently he could. He refused to speak to her after that. Finally, after another long, tearful phone call from Patty, Jack agreed to try to talk some sense into his friend for her.

It was the night before the prom. Luke was brooding in his living room. As had been the case with Patty, this time it was Luke's parents who were out of town. His older brother was away at college.

Jack came over, armed with a six pack of beer, not exactly sure what he would accomplish. They'd each had two beers apiece before Jack even broached the subject of Patty. At once Luke's face closed and he held up his hand in warning.

"Did she send you over here, Jack? Be honest."

"Luke, she's a mess. She's been crying on Emma's shoulder ever since you broke up with her. She missed half her finals. She's called me twice."

Luke shook his head. "Jesus. Since when did a relationship become the business of the entire high school?" Jack was stung by this remark. He and Emma were hardly the entire high school, but he said nothing. Luke continued, "You and me have been friends a long time. There's things about me and Patty you don't know."

"So tell me. I miss how we used to talk all the time. I miss our weekends before girls entered the picture."

"Yeah, me too. I think I was so caught up in the sex thing, I let things that really mattered to me get away." They were sitting side by side on the couch. Luke's voice grew earnest. "I feel like life is going too fast sometimes, you know? Like we're growing up too fast. I didn't just break up with Patty because she was cheating on me. That's not the first time she's been with Dominic, whatever she might have told you or Emma."

Jack was surprised by this, but made no comment. Luke added, "This whole thing with the engagement—that was all Patty. I didn't make a big deal of denying it, because I didn't want to embarrass her, but she knows I have no plans of marrying, certainly no time soon. I want to go to college. I want to travel the world. I want to explore all kinds of things."

His eyes narrowed and glittered as he turned toward Jack. He dropped his hand to Jack's thigh and reiterated, "All kinds of things."

The sound of a ringing telephone pulled Jack back into the present. He took a breath and shook away the old memories. What had happened between Luke and him was ancient history. "Water under the bridge," Emma would have said, though he'd never told her about that night. He'd never told a soul.

✧

The floor was down—broad planks of richly toned oak that gave the room a warm feel. Jack was again on the ladder, painstakingly removing the few damaged tin tiles and replacing them with new ones. He'd managed to match the pattern, a classic butterfly oak leaf motif.

"I found these in a kitchen supply shop next to a pool hall I sometimes go to. These are actually original tiles the guy found at an estate sale. You can't get much more authentic than that," he added with a satisfied smile.

The new cabinets and countertops, still wrapped in huge swaths of clear plastic wrap, had been delivered and were taking up most of the living room. Will realized with a sharp pang that at the rate Jack was going, within a week or so the work would be done, and Jack would be gone.

It had been three days since their shared lunch on the deck. While Jack continued to be pleasant and friendly, he gave no hint of interest in anything but a professional relationship between them.

Will, used to getting what he wanted especially where men were concerned, was at a loss. That evening at the gym, in a moment of weakness, he confided in Paul. They had just finished a vigorous game of racquetball and were sharing a cold drink in the gym's small café.

"So how goes it with your renovations?" Paul asked innocently.

"They're going fine," Will answered, feeling morose. "So fine they're almost done. Then he'll be gone."

"Then who'll be gone?"

"Jack. Jack Crawford, the handyman."

"So what do you care?" Paul slapped his forehead. "I get it

now. This is the dude I'm supposed to be jealous of. The married straight guy old enough to be your dad." He laughed.

"He's not old enough to be my dad," Will retorted, annoyed. "He's only fourteen years older than me. But yeah," his face fell as he added, "he's straight, all right."

"You know my theory on that."

"Yeah, yeah. You think no one's immune, I know. You think the whole human race is just one big sexual treasure chest, waiting to be plundered. You think we're all bisexual but society conditions us one way or the other. I know, I know."

"Well, experience has borne me out, hasn't it? Remember Jason?"

Jason was a sacker at the local supermarket, a Greek god, according to Paul. Paul had been smitten from the moment the guy asked him if he wanted paper or plastic. Engaged to be married, he'd nevertheless succumbed to Paul's persistent charms. They'd had a wild couple of trysts before Paul had lost interest and moved on.

Will knew the only reason Paul remained interested in him was precisely because they never got involved above the waist. They were, to use Paul's crude words, fuck buddies.

"I remember Jason, but he was just an impressionable kid. This guy is in his forties. He was married for a hundred years. No doubt he's set in his straight-and-narrow ways."

"Have you felt him out about it? Is he dating again? Seeing other women? If not, how come? Is he lonely? If you're determined to get in this guy's pants, maybe you could take the friend route." Paul motioned with his fingers, drawing quotations in the air around the word "friend". "You know, invite him out for lunch or drinks or something. Nothing too threatening. Get to know him outside the confines of his working for you. Be a sympathetic ear, if he needs one. Gently broach the subject of your own orientation. See how he reacts. Remember, most of what we want can be achieved if we just visualize the goal and go for it."

As Will started to protest, Paul held up a hand. "Hey, you never know until you try. Nothing ventured, nothing gained. Unless he's in that five percent of the population that is totally, one hundred percent straight, you've got a shot. Better than a shot, given your hot bod and dreamy green eyes. Shit, he's probably already jerking off at night, thinking of you."

Will shook his head. "Not everyone has your take on the world, Paul," he said with a laugh. Nevertheless, maybe Paul was right, at least about the way to approach him. He'd wait until the job was nearly complete—that way Jack would have an easy out if he wasn't interested.

That time came even sooner than he expected. Jack worked quickly and before they knew it the kitchen would be done. Will was delighted with how it was turning out, but anxious at the realization Jack would then be gone.

He hadn't shown up at all the day before, much to Will's disappointment. When the doorbell rang Will leaped up from his coffee and paper and hurried to answer it. Jack stood on the doorstep, a large bag in his hand.

"Here are the cabinet door handles, at last. I managed to find an oak leaf like we talked about, in burnished silver." He held one up for Will's inspection. "I think they'll be a nice touch, matching the ceiling tiles as they do."

They walked together to the kitchen and stood side by side, admiring the gleaming new appliances, the shiny white cabinets and black marble countertops. Jack held one of the knobs up to a cabinet and turned to Will for approval. Will nodded—they were perfect.

"This should wrap things up. I just want to put one more

coat of paint on the walls above the sink and cabinets and I should be done."

"You're really something," Will enthused. "I can't believe how well the whole thing has come together. You're a real Renaissance man of renovation."

Jack grinned. "I like what I do. I believe in putting everything you've got into whatever you do. Otherwise, what's the point?"

"What, indeed," Will murmured. He recalled Paul's remark that Jack might be lonely. Seizing a clue about his life from his earlier comment about the kitchen supply store, Will offered with studied casualness, "I was wondering, if you weren't busy later, maybe we could take in a game of pool. Grab a few beers, I don't know. Since I don't commute into the city anymore, I sometimes find myself at a loss during the evenings..." He trailed off. Jack would accept or refuse. He wouldn't press him if it was the latter. It would be a sign nothing was ever going to happen between them. He would let it go then and there. He would strike Jack and his brooding blue gray eyes and his powerful forearms and his thickly muscled thighs from his consciousness forever.

"Hey, that might be nice." Jack smiled. "I'd better warn you though, I wasted a good portion of my youth in pool halls."

"That's all right," Will countered. "I'm not competitive. Not when it comes to pool, anyway."

Now, why had he done that? Jack usually made it a rule not to get too friendly with people he worked for. It just seemed neater that way. His work life was in one compartment, his personal and social life in another.

Not that he had a social life anymore. The friends Emma and he had had were really her friends and their husbands, he realized in retrospect. He hadn't particularly minded any of them, but he'd never felt a real connection with any of them either.

When Emma had died, they'd made halfhearted attempts to include him in things, but when he'd declined they hadn't pressed, no doubt relieved. After a while, not a long one, they stopped calling and this had suited Jack.

Yet it was disconcerting to admit he'd never felt much of a connection with anyone, not since Luke. So why had he agreed to shoot pool with Will Spencer? Especially with Will, since he was pretty sure the guy was gay.

Jack had always considered himself open-minded, and told himself it didn't matter if Will were gay or straight. He liked the guy. He was smart and worldly, but he never talked down to Jack the way so many college-educated types did, just because Jack earned his living with his hands.

He actually reminded Jack of Luke—with his green eyes and wavy brown hair. Will was good-looking by anyone's standards. Even if he were gay, there was no way he was interested in Jack, who had a face only a mother could love. Not that Jack wanted him to be interested.

No. Since Luke he'd never looked at another man, and what had happened between them barely counted, since they'd been drunk and very, very young. He'd never looked at another woman since Emma, for that matter. Monogamy was hardwired into him, he supposed. He had promised to be faithful to Emma, and so he had been.

But now Emma was gone.

Though at forty-four he couldn't call himself young, he still had plenty of good years left ahead of him. It had been two years. Maybe it was time to start looking again—to start living again.

Luke's words from so long ago came back to him as an echo of what might have been. *I want to explore all kinds of things.* Then, as his hand had dropped to Jack's thigh, sending volts of electricity directly to Jack's groin, he'd repeated, "All kinds of things."

Maybe now, a lifetime later, Jack was at last ready to do the same.

They were on their second game of eight ball. The first game had been quick. Jack had allowed Will to break. Will scratched on his first shot. Jack proceeded to sink all his balls before Will got a second chance. Will hadn't really minded. He liked watching Jack bend over the table, his face twisted in concentration as he mentally calculated angles and trajectories, or whatever it was one calculated to hit the ball into a pocket.

Will broke again, this time at least managing to keep the cue ball on the table. Jack stood just behind him. "If you hold the cue stick like this," he said, reaching around behind Will and touching his wrist, "you'll have better control over it." He leaned closer, his chest against Will's back.

"Instead of hitting the ball with that jerking motion, it's better to stroke it, like this." As he spoke, he touched Will's elbow, gently guiding it forward to demonstrate. Will resisted the strong urge to lean back against Jack. He tried to concentrate on his game and did manage to do better than the first time, though Jack still easily beat him.

They ordered a pitcher of cola, which they carried, along with two frosted mugs, to a booth. They slid in on opposite sides. "Sorry I'm not much of a challenge," Will said apologetically.

"You were all right. You just need some practice. It's a matter of visualizing what you want and then making it happen."

Will grinned in spite of himself, harking back in his mind to Paul's similar comment. Could he just close his eyes and will Jack to step into his arms?

"What're you smiling about?" Jack asked, tilting his head.

"I was just thinking how great it would be if we could really do that. I mean, just close your eyes and wish and change the world."

"That would be nice," Jack said, smiling. "But that isn't what I meant. I meant you need to focus. To line your eye with the ball and visualize where it's going to go. It matters where you hit the ball, which side. It matters the force of the stroke and the angle at which you hit it. You have to think ahead, to see in your mind's eye where the ball will go, and how it will affect the setup for the next shot. I suppose you could say it's a metaphor for life—everything you do impacts what happens next."

"And sometimes," Will added, "it's just plain, blind luck."

"Sure," Jack agreed. "Though the longer I've lived, the more I think the harder we work for something, the luckier we get."

They drained their mugs and Jack filled them again, at home in his own environment. "I don't know about you, but I'm getting kind of hungry. They have good pizza here, if you like plenty of salty cheese and grease." Jack grinned.

Will, who favored feta, Greek olives and sun-dried tomatoes on sourdough pizza crust made in a wood-burning oven, lied. "My favorite."

Jack summoned a waitress with a gesture. As he ordered the pizza, she gave Will a long, lingering once over. He was used to this reaction from women and barely noticed her. Once she was gone, Will turned to Jack. "Thanks for coming out. I guess sometimes lately I get lonely."

As he'd hoped, Jack picked up the thread. He was definitely more open and relaxed now that the bill had been paid and they were no longer in a client relationship. "I get lonely too. Being married for so many years, it kind of conditions you to have someone around."

"I can imagine. You must really miss her."

"I do, though not necessarily in the way you might expect."

"What do you mean?"

"Well, we got married so young. Too young, really, to know what we were doing. Then we just kind of stuck with it. I was used to her, you see. And she to me. But I don't honestly know if what we had was true love or just habit."

"Huh." Will mulled this over. He was surprised Jack had admitted such a stark truth. He decided to press a little more. "Do you think you would have stayed with her if she'd, uh, if she was still around?" He felt the tips of his ears heat, afraid he'd upset Jack with his crass reminder she was dead.

Jack looked thoughtful, but not offended. "I've thought about that. Yes, I probably would have. Because how do you leave someone who relies on you? Who has relied on you all their adult life?" He lifted his mug and drank. "I think my sense of duty would have kept me with her. But since she's been gone I've had a lot of time to really think over my life. To take stock, I guess you'd say. I don't think there's much use in regretting the past, at least that's what I try to tell myself in my saner moments.

"Still, I can't help wondering what would have happened if things had been different..." He paused, staring off into the middle distance. Will would have given anything to be inside his head at that moment.

The pizza arrived, the aroma of tomato sauce and melted cheese making Will's mouth water. Circles of pepperoni with little pools of melted grease at their centers dotted the pie.

They each helped themselves to a piece and for a while they were silent as they ate. Jack finished his first piece and reached for a second. "So, what's next? Kitchen's done. Which room is next on your list? Those bathrooms could do with some work. I don't do much complicated plumbing but I know a few good, reliable guys we could use for the tough parts. We could draw up some plans for the master bath. I envision a hot tub and a steam shower, at the very least. You know, those fancy ones with fifty jets coming at you from all angles."

Will tried to fight the broad smile that threatened to spread over his face. Was the guy just after more business, or was he looking for a way to stay in Will's life? Was Paul's theory going to bear itself out?

Stop it. He just wants the work. It's nothing personal.

To test his theory, to prove to himself there was absolutely nothing between them but the chance of another job, Will said with an almost reckless abandon, "After the pizza, let's go back to my place. We could pick up some pastries from this great Italian bakery near my house and have dessert and coffee in my beautiful new kitchen."

He held his breath, waiting for Jack to refuse.

"They got cannoli? I'm a sucker for good cannoli."

"Yeah, they sure do," Will affirmed, though in fact he had no idea. This time he didn't fight his grin. He could feel it spread like sunlight over his face. His heart did a loop de loop as Jack smiled back.

Chapter Four

From his vantage point at the dining room table, Jack watched Will carefully measure and pour whole coffee beans into a fancy black and stainless steel coffee-making contraption that probably cost as much as his old pickup truck was worth. He was sure the coffee would taste fine, but doubted it would taste much different from the coffee he made in the old auto-drip machine he'd had for twenty years.

The coffee smelled wonderful as it started to brew. The cannoli sat piled on a plate on the table in front of him. Jack wanted to eat one—to just pop the whole thing into his mouth, but he waited for Will, not wanting to be impolite.

"Can I get the cream and sugar or something?" he asked, feeling antsy, not used to being waited on by someone other than Emma. For some reason, he couldn't seem to take his eyes off Will's body. His jeans fit like a comfortable second skin, molding along the curve of his ass down long, lean legs.

"No, I got it. Just hang on a second. I've got the coffee going now. Sometimes I think you need a license just to operate this damn thing." Will turned toward him and flashed a grin. Jack noticed, not for the first time, Will's movie-star-perfect smile. He had a dimple in his left cheek and his eyes sort of creased up into half moons when he grinned broadly, which he'd been doing a lot this evening, or so it seemed to Jack.

What am I doing here?

The question flashed into his brain and as it did, a part of Jack wondered why it had taken so long to get there. What exactly was he doing with a young, handsome gay man? Had they been on a date, for God's sake? Were they now going to finish the date with dessert and a good-night kiss? By coming back to Will's house, was he tacitly offering himself up for a homosexual encounter?

Jesus, cut it out. The word homosexual sounded so formal, so dated. So Will was gay, big deal. Was it a crime to have a gay friend? He had female friends, or he used to, he supposed, when Emma was around. If he was alone in the kitchen with one of them, did that necessarily mean sex was in the offing? No, it did not.

He and Will had become friends over the two weeks he'd worked on his kitchen. Will was easy to talk to. He understood about Emma, empathetic about Jack's self-imposed loneliness without making him feel self-conscious. Jack had to admit he liked how Will seemed to hang on his every word, awed by his renovation skills and his "artist's eye" as Will had called it. When he was with Will he didn't feel like just a handyman. He felt as if the work he was doing really mattered.

He surveyed the room, admiring his own handiwork. The marble countertops gleamed, the floor looked as if it had always been there, the appliances fit perfectly. He glanced up the ceiling, studying the oak leaf pattern pressed into the white tin. This kitchen, he thought proudly, could be featured in one of those home-improvement magazines.

Will moved to the table, carrying a tray with mugs, a pitcher of cream and a sugar bowl. "I'm going to have to have a big dinner party to show off my new kitchen."

Jack suddenly imagined this dining room table, which

seated eight, filled with Will's rich young friends—the up-and-coming movers and shakers of the financial community. Or maybe he'd have all gay men, GQ-model types, each one better looking than the last, lifting their champagne flutes, their little fingers extended as they lisped their toasts to one another before falling into a debauched orgy...

Come on, Crawford, get a grip.

Will left him a moment and this time returned with a bottle of Cognac and two brandy snifters. "I thought we could toast the new kitchen," he said as he set them on the table. He brought over the coffeepot and stood beside Jack as he filled each mug with aromatic, steaming coffee. As he leaned down, his arm brushed Jack's shoulder and the touch sent an inexplicable shiver down Jack's spine.

Will sat across from Jack and gestured toward the cannoli. "Please, help yourself. I didn't mean for you to wait."

Jack selected a cannoli and bit into the light, crunchy shell. The creamy cheese filling exploded like heaven on his tastebuds, and he closed his eyes, savoring its sweet ecstasy. When he opened his eyes to reach for his coffee, he found Will staring at him, those large green eyes focused like a cat on a mouse. He felt himself blushing, which was ridiculous.

Will uncorked the brandy and poured a healthy amount in each snifter. He held one out for Jack. Jack hesitated, but then took the glass, not wanting to be rude. He looked down at the rich, amber liquid and moved the glass, watching it swirl.

"Is something wrong?"

Jack glanced up at Will and said honestly, "It's been a while since I had hard liquor. I sort of fell into a rut the first few months after my wife died. I think I was coming to rely a little too much on alcohol to get me through the day, if you know what I mean."

"I didn't realize." Will held out his hand. "I can take these away if you like."

"No, no. I'd like to share a brandy with you. Enough time has passed now. I think I can drink responsibly."

"Fair enough." Will raised his glass toward Jack, who raised his in turn. "To my beautiful new kitchen. Thank you, Jack Crawford, for your meticulous, high-quality work and your vision. You truly are an artist."

Jack couldn't help but grin, both pleased and amused by the young man's abundant praise. "My pleasure," he mumbled. He tipped back the glass and swallowed the strong, slightly sweet spirit. It felt good burning down his chest.

"Another?" Will held up the bottle.

"Sure, what the hell?"

Will poured another several ounces into his glass. Jack ate two more cannoli and drank his coffee, which, he had to grudgingly admit, was actually quite a bit better than the stuff he made at home.

Will wasn't eating. He'd had one bite of his pastry and left it sitting on his dessert plate. His coffee mug was still nearly full. Instead he focused on his brandy, cupping the balloon glass in his hands as if using it to warm them. He looked anxious.

"You okay?" Jack asked.

"Me? Yeah. What do you mean? I'm fine."

Jack smiled, feeling his grin spread slow and easy over his face. He felt good. He knew he was drunk. He knew his defenses were down. He knew he should probably be leaving, but damn it, where the hell did he have to go? Back home to his empty house to watch TV or read or do the damn crossword puzzle out of the paper like some old man waiting to die?

He liked Will. He liked the way Will seemed genuinely

interested in the renovations, involved at each step. He'd enjoyed the evening playing pool and eating pizza. Boldly he stared at Will, who was looking down into his brandy glass. He liked the way Will's lips seemed to curve into a kind of Cupid's bow. He had a strong chin and jaw and straight brows over those very green eyes. He really did look like Luke. Or the Luke of days gone by. The Luke Jack remembered. The one who had touched his thigh, his face so earnest as he leaned forward, willing Jack not to pull away as their lips met…

"Jack? You okay?"

"What?" Jack jerked himself back to the present, focusing woozily on Will. "Yeah. Sorry. I think I had more to drink than I realized."

"Let's go sit on the sofa, why don't we? Unless you want more cannoli?" There were still two of the sweet, rich pastries on the plate.

Jack shook his head. "If I eat another one, I'll explode."

Will stood, taking his half-full brandy snifter with him. "A refresher?" he asked, pointing toward Jack's empty glass.

"No, no. I've had more than enough," Jack assured him. "I'll have a little more coffee though." He poured himself a cup and added some cream before following Will into the next room. He would finish the cup and hopefully sober up as a result.

Jack sat on the couch as Will put some music on the sound system. Will sat on the couch as well, though not near. Jack had half-expected Will to sit right next to him, to put his arm around him, to pull him close…

He realized with a sudden jolt he'd only assumed Will was gay. He'd made a stereotypical assumption, based on Will's appearance, his interest in the kitchen, his attention to artistic detail, the lack of a woman in the picture. What if he was totally off base? What if Will was as straight as he was?

How did one bring up something like that? Hint around about a girlfriend or ex-wife? Ask if he'd marched in the pride parade that year?

"You're grinning, Jack, but I don't know why," Will said with an answering half-smile.

Jack sat up and took a gulp of his coffee. "Listen, Will. I'm not used to all the brandy. That's my excuse." He offered a lopsided grin and barreled on. "I'm going to ask you straight out because I don't know how else to do it. Are you gay?"

Will, who had been sipping his brandy, sputtered into the glass. "What?"

Jack felt his face heat. God, he was a jerk. "I'm sorry. That was so out of line. It's just I realized I kind of assumed and well, tonight, I'm not exactly sure what's going on. I mean, if anything's going on, which I'm not saying anything is. I mean, you know. It's just..." *Save me from this ramble.*

Will complied to the silent plea. "Hey, calm down. It's okay. I just didn't expect the question. I guess I figured you knew."

"Then, you are?" Jack's mouth felt dry.

"Is this a fact-finding mission, or do you have a particular reason for asking?"

"I don't know," Jack mumbled, feeling suddenly much more sober. It was strange, for though he was obviously the senior of the two, he felt like a kid, confused and out of his ken.

Will scooted a little closer and turned toward Jack. "Look, I'm not going to lie to you. I really like you. A lot. But I know how things are. I didn't invite you out in order to hit on you. I genuinely enjoy your company. You're different from anyone I've ever known. You're wise and funny. You're humble even though you have every right to be very proud of the amazing work you do. I don't know how to explain this, and probably shouldn't even try, but something about you speaks to something inside me."

He shook his head and said, "I'm not saying that right. What I mean is, when you're around I somehow feel calmer. I tend to hold things too tight inside myself. I let stuff get sort of balled up and it eats at me. That's why I had to take a break from the work I was doing on Wall Street. I was letting it eat me up inside. But for some reason when you're around, that tension inside me eases. I feel a kindredness, something between us that sometimes, when my guard is down, I imagine you feel too. I have this crazy idea maybe we could explore it—together."

Jack stared at Will, completely at a loss for words. Will took a deep breath and blew it out. "Fuck. I wasn't going to do that. I'm *such* a jerk." He held his glass aloft. "I guess I had too much to drink too. You probably want to go now."

"No. I want to stay."

Every silent signal emanating from Jack seemed to say, "Kiss me." He was staring at Will with those intense, brooding eyes of his, his lips pressed tightly together, his hands twisting in his lap. Will was reminded suddenly of his first kiss with one Jane Cuthbert, when he was nine years old.

Every summer Will's father hauled them out of the city to a stay in a cottage in the Hamptons. That particular summer his father had helped him build, or more accurately had built a tree house for Will while he handed him tools and nails. It was really just a conglomeration of wood planks and two-by-fours but to his nine-year-old eyes it was a wonderful, secret lair in which he passed many happy hours.

Ten-year-old Jane, whose family rented the cottage next door, invited herself up but Will didn't mind. He was proud of his tree house and happy to show it off, even to a girl.

"Do you want to kiss me?" Jane asked. She was a pretty girl, with long blonde braids framing a pixie face.

"Sure." Why not? They were sitting cross-legged facing one another, Will's pile of comic books between them. He leaned forward and she screwed up her eyes and pursed her lips in an exaggerated gesture. When his lips touched hers, she twisted her head violently away.

"You don't want to?" Will asked, confused.

"I want to. I'm just scared. It's my first time, you see."

"Mine too." Will shrugged. What was the big deal about touching lips anyway? He tried again and this time she stayed still. After a moment he pulled back and she opened her eyes and grinned at him.

"Now we're boyfriend and girlfriend." She was triumphant.

"Whatever." He was noncommittal.

Will wondered if Jack would turn away if he tried to kiss him. *I want to. I'm just scared.*

Will hadn't really been sure what he hoped to accomplish by inviting Jack back to his place. Well, that wasn't entirely true. A part of him, the wishful thinking totally unrealistic part of him, held some kind of fantasy that upon entering the house, Jack would press Will against the front door and pull at his clothing, desperately kissing his mouth as he fumbled with the zipper of Will's jeans. They would slide together to the floor, pulling off each other's clothes in their rush to feel the naked press of flesh against flesh.

The saner part of him thought maybe they could talk. Perhaps, his inhibition lowered a bit by alcohol, Jack might not be offended if Will probed a little, if he tried to gauge if there was the slightest chance of anything happening between them.

He hadn't bolted just now, so that was a good sign. He had

been honest, and said he didn't know what he wanted. While that was hardly a declaration of love, or even interest, at least it wasn't an outright rejection.

"Would you like to go outside? It's such a nice night. We could sit on the deck."

Jack stood quickly. "That's a good idea. Yes, some fresh air would be good." He followed Will to the kitchen and out the back door, Will carrying his snifter, Jack his coffee mug. They stood for a moment, looking up at the sky sparkling with stars. Will stared up into the clear spring night. He still wasn't used to seeing so many stars, having grown up in the city.

"It's like someone threw a bucket of diamonds up there. I know that's cliché, but that's what it looks like."

"Twinkle, twinkle, little star," Jack said with a grin. Will was relieved the tension between them had eased.

They sat side by side on two cushioned reclining chairs set on the edge of the deck, a small table between them. Jack leaned back and looked up, pointing. "See that? There's Orion's Belt, those three bright stars in a row."

Will followed his finger, saying, "Orion the hunter and his faithful dog, Sirius. I used to think it was spelled serious, like the mood. My dad used to take me up to the roof of our apartment building on clear nights. He had this old brass telescope. I actually have it now—it's up in the attic. I should pull it down sometime."

"Wow, no kidding. I love stars and constellations. I used to be able to find all the famous ones and some not so famous. At least I imagined I could." He pointed again. "See that bright kind-of-orange-colored star up to the left of the belt? That's—"

"Beetle Juice." Will laughed. "A nasty drink made of ground-up bugs."

Jack laughed too. "Betelgeuse—a favorite in crossword

puzzles."

They stared again at the sky, their silence now companionable. Will was glad he hadn't done anything stupid like try to make a move back in the house. Jack was still here, and that in itself was enough. He glanced shyly over at the older man, who continued to scan the heavens. What would it be like to taste his lips?

Jack, oblivious of Will's secret yearning, pointed upward. "Look way over there. I'm pretty sure that's Leo the Lion, though for the life of me, I've never seen anything in it resembling a lion."

Will stared at the little blob of stars he thought Jack was pointing to. He couldn't see a thing there either, but then he never saw shapes among the stars. He always figured he lacked the imagination. Still, it was fun to find something to share with Jack, something he clearly enjoyed. "I'm glad you're here, Jack. I'm glad we're becoming friends."

"I am too, Will. It's been a long time since I've spent any time with anyone, except when I'm working. I guess I've become something of a hermit. If my little sister didn't make me come over for Sunday dinner, I might never get out. I should be honest with you, though. I don't really know what I'm doing here. I like you. I've never really known any gay guys before."

"Yes you have."

"Pardon?"

"You've known them. You just didn't know you knew them. They didn't let you know because they didn't want you to judge them, or get them fired, or whatever it is they feared you might do if you found out."

Will tried to keep the bitterness from his tone. "Sure, we live in more enlightened times than the bad old days, when a man was burned to death for his sexual orientation, or jailed for it, or beaten to death by horrified heterosexuals. Or at any rate those things are against the law now, at least in this country. But don't fool yourself that gay men or women feel free to come out—to admit with pride they are what they are.

"It takes courage, still, to tell the world to fuck itself if it has a problem. Not everyone is accepting, as I'm sure you know. Some people still labor under the false assumption it's something we choose, like a career or a new car. Did you choose to be straight? Did you choose to be right-handed?"

Will stopped himself. "Look, I'm sorry. I tend to get on a soapbox. You're a really cool guy, and I appreciate you may be totally nonjudgmental and just fine about me being gay. I'm oversensitive, I guess. I don't hide my orientation, but neither do I make a point of flaunting it. I never took a date, for example, to any work function. I'm discreet, though sometimes it pisses me off that I have to be. And I get mad at myself that I continue to lay low, to be cool, to leave them guessing.

"Now that I'm not in that cutthroat work environment, I have less to lose. Still, I have to be careful. There are a lot of jerks out there still ready to beat me to a pulp just because of my existence. I don't know if you can imagine what that's like—how it colors the way you perceive the world around you."

Jack was watching him, an earnest expression on his face. "That sounds really hard. I guess I never really thought about it in those terms. I wish things were different. If it's any comfort, I don't feel that way. I believe people should be free to express themselves as they truly are."

Will nodded, knowing he should probably shut up, but now that the floodgates were open, he couldn't. "Sometimes I think we're all really bisexual, to one degree or another. I mean, look at girls. Girls are permitted to cuddle and kiss, to walk hand in hand and tell each other they love each other. Boys are strongly discouraged from behaving this way, but who's to say the impulse isn't there? I think humans seek comfort and love where they can find it, but our society discourages one sex over the other from expressing it, except in very defined, prescribed ways. I mean, think about it. Really think back. Was there ever someone you felt strongly about? A guy, I mean. Someone you might have had feelings for that seemed to go beyond what society dictated was proper?"

Jack slowly nodded. Somewhat surprised, Will went on. "I bet you squashed those feelings down. I bet you didn't allow yourself to explore them because they were wrong. They were *inappropriate* so you shut them down, locked them away or discarded them altogether."

"Slow down, Will. Take it easy." Jack touched Will's forearm. Will took a breath and let it out with a sharp, nervous laugh.

"God, I'm sorry. Just totally ignore me, will you?"

"I don't want to ignore you. I think what you're saying is important." His hand was still on Will's arm. Will looked down and, predictably, Jack pulled it away.

"Will, I'm not really sure what's going on right now. I do know I've had a little too much to drink and my brain is kind of fuzzy. I was married a lot of years and I guess I haven't really thought one way or the other about your notion of people being conditioned this way or that. I never thought of myself as gay."

Embarrassed, Will blurted, "I never meant to imply—"

"Now hold on, relax," Jack interrupted him. "I said I never thought of myself that way. But honestly, I've never thought much about my feelings, period. It's really only since Emma died that I've taken the time to ruminate about weighty things like life and death and why we're here and what we should be getting out of life. Being around you these past weeks, well..."

Jack flushed and looked down. He looked up again, meeting Will's eyes. "It's been great. You make me feel valued for my work and even more importantly, valued as a person.

"I enjoyed working on your kitchen. It was gratifying to see you take such an active interest every step of the way. You made me see things through your eyes and remember why I do this in the first place."

Will started to respond but Jack kept on. "I liked when you told me about your investment business, even though I didn't really get it." He smiled shyly. "I liked playing pool with you, even though you suck at it." His smile broadened into a grin. "I liked eating pizza with you and watching you make coffee in that fancy machine of yours. I like the way you're so serious and impassioned about gay rights. I like you, Will.

"I have no idea what that means in relation to us, if it means anything at all. My wife always said my tongue waggled without consulting my brain when I'd had a few too many, and I'm sure she'd say it this time too. I just kind of wanted to get all that out there, I guess. I have no idea where we go from here."

Neither, Will realized, did he.

Chapter Five

The moon was rising, its reflected light illuminating Jack's features. He seemed to be waiting for Will's response. Will could feel the underlying tension between them and wasn't sure how much of it was sexual, how much of it brandy and wishful thinking.

When he didn't respond immediately Jack turned his face away, again staring up at the star-filled sky. Will felt as if he'd let a pivotal moment pass but he didn't know how to get it back. He'd been so focused on his own unrequited feelings for the older man, he hadn't been prepared for Jack's tumbling torrent of words.

He sipped his brandy and tried to collect his thoughts. It was pretty obvious Jack was drunk, at least drunk enough to speak so freely, to say things he might regret when sober. While Will desperately wanted to question him about what he'd said, at the same time he didn't want to press, to embarrass him, to make him regret his uncharacteristic volubility.

I like you, Will.

Will took another sip of brandy, forbidding himself from attaching too much meaning to that simple statement. Unbidden, in his mind's eye he saw himself lean over and take Jack into his arms. He closed his eyes, lowering his face to Jack's for their first, perfect kiss...

The image shifted, and instead of Jack offering himself in sweet surrender, Will's fevered imagination conjured him standing with his fist clenched and raised, delivering a sharp right that knocked Will on his ass.

Will shook his head but couldn't quite erase the unsettling fantasy. He decided to quit while he was ahead. "Hey, it's been a really great evening. I don't know about you, but I've had a fair amount to drink and maybe neither of us is thinking as clearly as he'd like. I think it's best if we called it a night. Do you want another cup of coffee before you drive? How far do you have to go, anyway?"

Jack was clearly nonplussed. He stood abruptly, nearly toppling the chair behind him. "I live about twenty minutes from here. As to coffee, no thanks. If I have another cup I'll be up all night." His voice was gruff, his face, a moment before so open and earnest, had closed.

Will felt as if someone had attached lead weights to his body. He could hardly move, overcome with the sinking feel he'd ruined everything. If only he could read Jack better. If only he had the balls to be direct, to take what he wanted, what *maybe* Jack wanted too.

Stiffly, Jack thrust out his hand. Will gripped the offered hand, wishing somehow everything he was feeling could be magically imparted through touch. He held on too long and Jack pulled away.

Trying to keep his voice light and neutral, Will said, "I had a great time, Jack. Thank you—for everything."

"Yeah. Me too. Catch you later."

Though it was well after midnight, Jack sat up in his workroom, wood shavings piled around him as he worked on the curving leg of a rocking chair he'd been building. The process of working the wood with his tools relaxed him, as it always did. It was more than an act of creation—it was a kind of meditation. He'd done some of his best thinking while working with a chisel and a lathe.

He had driven home carefully, deliberately going ten miles below the speed limit so no cop would be tempted to stop him. He could still barely believe he'd had the nerve to make that long-winded speech about how much he liked Will and liked being with him.

Even while he was blathering on, he knew he should shut up but he couldn't seem to stop himself. What had he expected Will to say? To do? What had he hoped for? He honestly didn't know.

He hadn't expected Will's rather abrupt dismissal. He felt first let down, and then humiliated and embarrassed by what seemed like a rejection, or at the very least a rebuff. Whatever strange heat he imagined had been building between them had cooled. Had it only been one-sided? Just because he'd confirmed Will was gay, had he then gone on to incorrectly assume Will was somehow interested in him?

Jack laughed bitterly. Why would a handsome young guy like that be interested in him? He'd obviously been drunker than he'd thought, and misread whatever cues Will had been sending.

He was lucky Will had nipped whatever had been going on in the bud. He'd made the right decision for them both. Whatever he was feeling, he wasn't yet ready to confront it, especially not in front of Will.

Jack set his woodworking tools down and lay on the floor in

the middle of the sawdust and wood scraps. He stared up at the ceiling, seeing a face from long ago.

His mind veered, as it had often done lately, back to that fateful night. He picked up the thread of his recollection from the week before, and realized now with a flash of clarity it was Will's presence in his life that had rekindled the memories of Luke, even before he'd been aware of their mutual attraction.

Then, as tonight, Luke and he had both had plenty to drink. Emma and Jack were still virgins. They did engage in some heavy petting, and, though he would have been mortified to admit it, he'd come in his pants more than once while they'd kissed and fumbled beneath their clothing, parked along the side of the road in his parents' car after a night at the movies.

That night Luke and Jack talked about girls, love, life and their futures, the beer loosening their speech and lowering their inhibitions. When Luke put his hand on Jack's thigh it was almost like the world held its breath, waiting to see which direction Jack would take.

Jack wondered how different his life might have been if he'd rebuffed Luke. If he'd pushed him away from the start, before things went too far. Then Jack wouldn't have had anything to prove.

But he hadn't.

I want to explore all kinds of things. Luke's meaning became clear as he gently squeezed his best friend's leg. It was late May and they were both wearing shorts. Luke's hand on his leg was warm, his fingers stroking Jack's skin.

Jack's cock responded before the rest of him did as he locked eyes with the green-eyed boy who had been his best friend and closest confidant for so many years. When Luke leaned forward, parting his lips, Jack had moved forward as well.

When they kissed he'd thought his heart might actually thump right through his chest, it was beating so hard. He knew he wasn't gay—he knew Luke wasn't either. And yet the kiss felt so right, so good.

Unlike Emma, who kissed eagerly, almost sloppily, Luke took his time, teasing Jack with his tongue, drawing it seductively over Jack's lips before slipping its tip between them. He held Jack's face, cradled in his hands as he suckled and tasted Jack's mouth.

Jack touched his lips, even now recalling the heat of that kiss. He hadn't protested as Luke pulled at his shorts, reaching past the waistband to find his rising cock. Emma had touched him like this too, but her grip had been clumsy and unsure. Jack leaned back, telling himself they were drunk and would forget this. He let Luke fondle and massage him. It felt good. Better than good.

Luke stroked him, gently at first, and then with more friction as Jack stiffened in his hand. Within minutes he knew he was going to come. He didn't want to ejaculate in his pants, in Luke's hand. "Luke, stop, I'm going to—"

"I want you to," Luke cut him off, his fingers drawing Jack past the edge of resistance. "Come on, you know you want it. We both want it. Don't fight it. Be honest with yourself for once in your life."

"Luke, stop..." Jack's protest weakened as Luke tightened his grip, relentlessly pulling and stroking Jack's stiff shaft.

All at once he came in Luke's hand, gasping as he shuddered with release. He fell back against the sofa, trying to catch his breath. What the hell had just happened? What the goddamned hell had just happened between him and his best friend? Between him and another guy?

Now that he'd orgasmed, his reason was no longer so

clouded by lust and he began to recoil in shock. Luke was watching him with narrowed eyes, his own cock still bulging in his shorts.

"Do it for me," Luke whispered urgently. "Make me come too." He grabbed Jack's hand and pressed it against his erection. Jack pulled it away. He didn't feel drunk anymore. He felt ashamed.

"Luke, *no*. I can't."

"Sure you can. It's easy. Come on. I did you. Do me. There's nothing wrong with it. There's nothing wrong with the way we feel about each other."

"I don't know what you're talking about. *We* don't feel any way about each other. We're friends. Buddies. That's all we've ever been. I don't know what the hell just happened but it sure wasn't something *I* planned."

Luke held his a gaze a moment and then looked sharply away, his face flushing crimson. He crossed his arms over his chest. "You didn't seem to mind so much when my hand was on your dick." His voice came out a sneer though even then Jack knew it was to hide the pain of his rejection. Hotly, he continued, "You're in denial, Jack. You've always been in denial about us. I thought once we were older, especially now that we're about to get the fuck out of this town, we could be honest with each other and with ourselves. I guess I was stupid to think that. You're as repressed and hung up as all the other assholes."

Deeply stung, Jack retorted, "I don't know what the hell you're talking about. We're both dating girls. Now suddenly we're supposed to be gay lovers? I don't think so."

"Get out. Go. Just leave me alone." Luke's voice was hard, his eyes bright with unshed tears. Jack knew at that moment they could never be friends again. With a heavy heart and a confused mind he left Luke's house.

He never told anyone what happened.

The next night he'd gone all the way with Emma, mostly, he knew now, to prove to himself he was straight. Unfortunately, though he'd pulled out and she'd assured him it was the wrong time of the month, once was enough to get her pregnant.

The course of his life was set in that instant. He did the right thing, or what had seemed like the right thing at the time.

Luke avoided him the last month of school and left for Europe after his last exam, not even staying for graduation. That was the last he'd seen of him.

He managed to put Luke from his mind, blotting out the entire incident for days at a time. He was straight, he was getting married, he was going to be a father. As his own father crudely pointed out to him when he'd confessed Emma was pregnant, he'd made his choice with his dick and now he'd pay the price for the rest of his life.

Jack had been raised to believe men were strong. They handled what life hurled at them with stoicism and fortitude. Whatever came their way, they sucked it up and dealt with it. Feelings didn't enter into it. Real men were never prey to fear or anxiety. Nor did they have desires, longings, passions or needs.

What a crock of shit that had turned out to be. What a lie. It took raising his own boys to realize just how stultifying and stunting such a macho attitude could be. At least with his sons, he'd encouraged them to express themselves honestly. He never told them big boys don't cry, as his parents had drilled into him when he was little, defenseless and scared.

Jack inhaled the sweet scent of sawdust and sighed. A single tear trickled down his cheek. Yes, he'd paid the price for that one night. He'd paid it a thousand times over. Yet it hadn't been a bad life. They'd raised two wonderful sons. Emma and he had been happy in their way. No, there had never been fireworks. His heart had never pounded as it had when Luke had kissed him. But he'd done the right thing.

Only now things were different, weren't they? He no longer had children to support, a wife to be faithful to. He was a free man. His own man. He could do what he wanted, as long as he was discreet.

Was he ready at last to explore the potential Luke had tried to offer him so long ago? Could he find the courage to let himself be vulnerable with another man?

Was Will that man?

Slowly he sat up and wiped the tear from his cheek. He ran his fingers through his thick hair and sighed. He had no idea what to do next.

"When you don't know what to do," his mother was fond of saying, "do nothing at all." That seemed like sound advice at the moment. He'd go to sleep and when he woke maybe things would be clearer.

Will awoke with a start, his body jerking in response to a half-remembered dream. He was sitting in his living room, an empty brandy glass still clutched in one hand. After he sent Jack away he'd proceeded to pour himself way too much brandy and drink it all, cursing himself all the while.

I had him. He was reaching out to me. And I rebuffed him. I sent him home like we were characters in some stupid romantic comedy from the fifties. Doris Day and Rock Hudson. Now he'll go home, sober up and thank God he got out of that one. I'll never hear from him again. I'm such a fucking idiot.

Will sighed and pressed his hands to his head, which was throbbing dully. Wearily he stood and made his way to the kitchen. He poured himself a glass of water from the new faucet Jack had helped him pick out and stood silently admiring the space.

Jack was more than a handyman, more than a carpenter. He was an artist. The room was elegant, functional and pleasing to the eye. One would never have looked at the burly, masculine Jack and assumed he was capable of such artistry. Will realized he was holding on to a stereotype in reverse—assuming a straight man like Jack wouldn't be capable of creating something beautiful.

Will drank the glass of water and poured another. Yes, he'd sent Jack away but, though he'd maybe lost an opportunity, he knew he had done the right thing. Any potential erotic feelings Jack was experiencing were too tentative to be taken advantage of while he was under the influence of alcohol. He might have been able to squeeze a one-night something out of it, but that wasn't what he wanted.

For whatever reason, he had to admit he wanted something more with Jack. Unlike Paul and all the other sex partners he'd had over the years, he felt a connection with Jack he couldn't explain. It made no sense when he tried to analyze it—Jack wasn't particularly handsome, he was too old, he was straight, or even if he wasn't, he came with a lot of baggage to shuck off before they could really have a meaningful relationship. Why would Will want to bother with someone like that? Why waste his time and energy? He could have his pick of men—why choose one so unlikely?

Why indeed? What made a person fall in love? Was it really something so simple as the way the other person smiled when you talked? The way he stroked the wall before applying paint, feeling for any hidden roughness he would sand away? Was it the way he'd touched Will's elbow as he stood close behind him at the pool table, guiding him with a gentle, sure touch that spoke of his quiet self-assurance? Was it his scent, a sexy combination of male essence and whatever soap he used, mixed with the fresh laundry scent of his faded, soft denim work shirts?

Am I in love?

Surely it was too soon to say. Will knew he was in lust. He knew he wanted to explore Jack's newfound interest, if that's what it was. He was dying to pick up the phone and call him—just to see if he got home okay, if he was okay with what they'd talked about. He looked at his watch. Two a.m. was a little late to be checking, seeing as he'd sent the guy away hours before.

With a sigh, he hauled himself off to bed.

In the morning a single beam of light fell onto Jack's face, waking him. Before he was fully conscious he knew something had changed. Something had happened that made him feel different, though still in a semi-sleep state, he couldn't recall what it was.

He became aware of the chirping of birds outside his bedroom window. He sat up and opened his eyes, squinting in the bright sunlight to see two robins, their red breasts proudly puffed as they whistled their springy duet. Jack smiled. He'd always regarded seeing robins as a sign of good luck.

He glanced at the clock. It was after nine. He rarely slept this late. Must have been all that brandy. The night returned to him with a flash, scrolling across his brain like a silent movie. He lay back against the pillows and put his hands behind his head. Just what exactly had gone on last night?

He tried to recall Will's precise words. *I feel a kindredness, something between us that sometimes I imagine you feel too. I have this crazy idea maybe we could explore it—together.*

Men didn't say that sort of thing to one another. Not straight men, anyway. Yet when Will had said it, Jack hadn't recoiled, though he hadn't known how to respond. He felt the same way, really. At least as far as feeling a certain connection—an easiness he rarely felt with anyone.

Will had crept up on him. He'd slipped past Jack's usual reserve with his disarming admiration and open friendliness. Was that all it was? Was Jack merely lonely? Was Will the first person to bother, since Emma had been gone, to push past his defenses?

Or was there something more? Did he find Will attractive? As a man? As a potential...lover?

Just the word made Jack flush, though he was alone in the room in his empty house. Did he flush because the idea repulsed him? Or because it excited him? Was he finally ready, twenty-six years after the fact, to explore whatever homoerotic feelings he might have buried beneath a lifetime of denial?

Jack got up and went into the bathroom, his bladder for the moment distracting him from his ruminations. After he peed, he turned on the shower and waited for the spray to heat as he shucked off his pajama bottoms and underwear.

He stared at himself in the bathroom mirror. What could Will possibly see in him? He was in his forties, the hair on his chest going gray, the laugh lines around his eyes pronounced, as were the grooves along either side of his mouth.

His body was still strong and firm, as a result of steady, hard physical work all his life. No gym workouts and tennis games to keep in shape, not for Jack Crawford. He'd built his muscles through the labor of his back and the sweat of his brow. He grinned at himself, aware for a horrible moment he sounded just like his father.

He turned sideways, consciously holding in his stomach and thrusting out his chest. Then he laughed out loud. He was being ridiculous—acting as vain as any insecure kid.

He climbed into the shower and soaped up his body and his hair, his mind returning to Will. Will's body was lean and firm—the body of an athlete. He was definitely good-looking—almost too good-looking, Jack thought. The kind of man whose face you'd see in an ad for men's cologne or fine Italian loafers.

Will had the look of an aristocrat, that's the word Jack was groping for. He was young, rich and smart. Why in the hell was he interested in Jack?

Was he interested in Jack?

Will might have meant only and precisely what he'd said—that he liked and admired Jack. That didn't mean he wanted to have anything more, did it? Just because he was gay didn't mean he wanted to jump into bed with every guy he came into contact with.

Jack rinsed in the hot spray and soaped himself up again, this time lingering over his cock and balls. He sighed with pleasure as his cock elongated and hardened beneath his fingers. He closed his eyes, lifting his face to the hot spray as he massaged his shaft.

Will... Despite himself, Jack saw those brilliant green eyes, fixed so intently upon him. He felt for one ridiculous heart-stopping moment Will was actually there, watching him stroke himself in the shower.

Would Will like to watch such a thing? Jack flushed at the thought but tried not to censor himself from thinking it. Did Will have sexual fantasies about him? Was he way off the mark about Will's feelings for him? After all, he'd only said he liked him. He'd said he enjoyed spending time with him. Yet when he had tried to respond in kind, admittedly in a clumsy, drunken ramble, Will had sent him away—dismissed him. Though part of him was relieved, it rankled nonetheless.

"My God, give it a rest, Crawford," Jack said aloud. "For all I know, the guy has zero interest, no intentions. Here I am, gearing up for some kind of gay encounter and Will has probably forgotten the whole thing. Jesus, I'm pathetic."

He forced himself to think of a naked woman as he finished jerking himself off. Just as he ejaculated his libido got the better of his conscious mind, thrusting the image of Will, bent over the pool table, his hair falling into his eyes, his lips parted as he prepared for a shot...

Jack finished his shower and roughly toweled himself dry. If only he hadn't finished the job at Will's place already. He prided himself on working steady and fast—it was a big reason he got repeat business, maybe the main reason. He had two jobs lined up for next week, though neither would take more than a day or two. After that, maybe he could call Will, invite himself over with some plans for Will's master bathroom. It could definitely use some renovation...

Wait a minute. What was he thinking? Jack never solicited business. He let it come to him. If Will wanted more work done, he had Jack's number. He wasn't about to foist himself on the guy just because they'd maybe spoken a little too freely after a little too much to drink.

If Will wanted to see him again, Will could call. Will, after all, had been the one to send him away. Let him call him back—if that's what he wanted. And if he didn't, well, that was that. Jack had been doing fine on his own these past two years. There was no reason to suppose he couldn't go on just as he had been for the next twenty.

Jack went about his business, making himself breakfast, eating it in front of the TV as he watched the Friday morning news, washing the few dishes and putting them in the rack to dry. He had a small job that afternoon—some finishing touches on a sunroom he'd built on a house not far from Will's. Then the weekend loomed.

As he poured himself a second cup of coffee an uninvited thought slipped into his head. *What if you wait for him to call, but he doesn't? Will you let this second chance slip away like you did the first?*

He had no answer.

Chapter Six

"Jack, you do *such* nice work. Your wife is so lucky to have such a *handy* man." Mandy Williams, an attractive woman in her late forties with perfectly dyed blonde hair, large blue eyes and rather too much makeup and jewelry clattered toward Jack on very high-heeled sandals.

The thick platinum wedding band and huge diamond on her ring finger left little doubt as to her marital status, but that hadn't stopped her from flirting, or attempting to flirt, with Jack since he'd arrived to finish the molding in her new sunroom.

He was used to women coming on to him over the years, and had always successfully rebuffed them, usually with a reference to his wife. This time he hadn't mentioned a wife but when she brought one up, he didn't disabuse her of the notion.

He was standing on the middle rung of a ladder, using a nail gun to secure a section of the ornate molding she'd decided on, after he'd already put up her first selection, which he'd personally preferred. Still, it was her dollar, and if she wanted to spend it having him put up and take down molding, that was her decision.

She came up directly behind him, standing so close he could smell her perfume. "Do you think she'd lend you to me, Jack? Just for a little while? Hmmm?" Her voice was low and sensual, its tone both insinuating and confident. He smiled to himself, wondering how many other hired hands she'd seduced over the years while her husband was off earning the sizable income it must take to maintain this suburban mansion.

She moved closer, her surgically enhanced breasts pressing up hard against the backs of his legs. He was surprised at himself—at how little her attempts at seduction moved him. He was pretty sure he could step down from that ladder and take her in his arms right then if he wished. He could follow her to her bedroom and fall into her king-sized bed and fuck her if he wanted.

He had absolutely no desire to do that. What he really wanted to do was finish this job and check his cell phone for messages. He'd left it in the truck by accident and hadn't realized it until he was in the middle of the job.

Maybe he'd call Will himself—apologize for his stupid drunken monologue of the night before. First he needed to head this one off at the pass.

"She's pretty darn jealous, my wife." He turned back to smile down at Mrs. Williams. "I imagine Mr. Williams feels the same way about you."

"Call me Mandy." She blinked up at him with long curling lashes as she slid the tip of her tongue suggestively along her full lower lip. "And no, he doesn't care what I do when he's not around. We have an—understanding."

Jack shot the last nail into the edge of the molding and climbed down from the ladder, forcing the woman to step back. He decided to act as if he hadn't heard her. "That should do it. The room is done at last." He glanced pointedly at his watch. "I'm sorry to run, but I have another job I need to be getting to—"

Mandy gripped his bare forearm. "Don't go. Please." The yearning in her face, the loneliness, was so palpable Jack found himself blushing, not for himself but for her. She barely knew him—they'd exchanged only a few words before today. He understood she didn't want him per se, but just a warm body—someone to hold and admire her, someone to fill the emptiness she must feel to proposition the handyman.

"Mrs. Williams, I—"

"Mandy." Her grip tightened, her long red fingernails grazing his skin.

"Mandy." Gently he uncurled her fingers from his arm and stepped back. "You're a beautiful woman. I just don't do that sort of thing. If I did, you'd be first on the list."

Mandy threw back her head and laughed, a high musical peal, though there was no joy on her face. "Well, at least you're gallant. I'll give you that." Her mouth curved down, making her suddenly look her age. "Faithful to little wifey to the bitter end," she sneered. Tossing her blonde hair back, she sniffed. "Well, that's your problem, not mine. I've got the plumber coming later."

It took Jack a moment to understand the implication of this statement. Mrs. Williams' voice was cold. "What do I owe you?"

"You're paid in full, ma'am. Your husband paid me last week."

"Oh Jesus, so it's *ma'am* now. Get out. Go on. Just go."

Jack went.

He meant to drive home but found himself instead driving in the direction of Will's place. The cell phone sat beside him in the cab, no missed calls or voice messages in evidence. Maybe he'd freaked Will out with his drunken declarations of affection. He could barely remember what he'd said now, but he knew he'd waxed on ad nauseam about how much he liked Will and liked doing things with Will and liked being with Will. He had probably sounded like a goofy teenager. No wonder Will had sent him home.

Well, he'd put it to rights. He took a detour as he neared Will's neighborhood, stopping at the Italian bakery Will had taken him to the night before. He pointed at the empty cannoli shells behind the glass. "I'll take six of those, please."

His mouth watered as the woman squeezed the fresh sweetened ricotta from a pastry tube into the delicate fried wafers. She placed them in a small white box and beamed at him as he paid for his purchase.

"You were here last night. I remember you." She pointed in his direction with an empty cannoli shell. "You like my cannoli. You're a good boy." Jack grinned at her use of the word boy though he supposed it was all relative. She looked close to eighty, her small dark eyes nearly lost in folds of wrinkles, thinning white hair pulled back in a bun, revealing strips of bald scalp.

Her smile was friendly, her eyes twinkling with pleasure as she watched Jack lift a cannoli from the box and take a bite, his eyes closing in ecstasy. Her accent was thickly Italian and gravelly with age. "You can't even wait to get it home, eh? You save some for that handsome boy you had with you last night, okay?"

Jack felt his cheeks heat, though he doubted she considered the two of them lovers. Not that they were. Jack shook his head. He was going to drive himself insane with all this nonsense.

As Jack drove, he again glanced at his cell phone on the

seat beside him, wondering if he should give Will a call before just showing up. He might not be home. Or worse, he might be home with someone else.

Jack slowed as he turned onto Will's street, still trying to decide if he should call first. As luck would have it, Will was in his front yard, kneeling in front of one of the flowerbeds pulling up weeds. Deciding this was a good omen, Jack pulled his truck into the driveway and cut the engine.

The sun was warm in a clear blue sky, and Will had taken off his shirt. He turned at the sound of the truck. When he recognized Jack, his face broke into a radiant smile and he waved. He stood, brushing the dirt from the knees of his jeans. Jack couldn't help but admire his broad bare shoulders and well-defined pecs and abs.

He climbed out of the truck and walked toward the garden. Will met him at the driveway. "Hey there. I was going to call you later. I assume you got home okay last night? I felt bad afterwards, sending you home with maybe too much alcohol in your system. I would have called this morning but I, well to tell you the truth, I chickened out." He grinned sheepishly and looked down at his bare feet.

Jack didn't know how to respond to this. Instead he held out the box of pastry. "I brought more cannoli. I have to confess, I bought them more for me than for you."

Will laughed and took the box. "Hey, that's okay. Come inside. I'll just get cleaned up and we can have an afternoon sugar-fest. I'll put on a pot of coffee."

Jack followed Will into the house, feeling happy and relieved. Will didn't seem put out to see him. In fact he seemed very happy. He wondered about Will's comment about chickening out, but decided he would find out in due time, if he was supposed to know.

"You know, about last night—"

"What I said last night—"

The two of them spoke in unison, processed what the other said and then laughed. "You go first," Will said.

"No, I want to hear what you have to say. Please."

Will nodded. This had to be harder for Jack than for himself, he realized. He, at least, was very comfortable in the terrain of homosexual encounters, having been gay and aware of it since he began having sexual feelings.

Though he doubted Jack was ready to declare his sudden conversion to Will's side of the tracks, his very presence today, unsolicited and without the excuse of work, said as much as the way he kept shyly glancing Will's way when he thought Will wasn't looking.

"I just wanted to say I really enjoyed spending time with you last night. I felt really bad though about the way it ended. I mean, I got the feeling you thought I wanted to get rid of you. In fact, that was the furthest thing from my mind.

"The truth is"—Will swallowed, thinking *now or never*, as he plunged on—"I wanted you to stay too much. I knew if you stayed, with the amount we'd had to drink, I might do something really stupid and scare you away.

"That was the last thing I wanted. You said a lot of things—things you might not have said otherwise, things you may not even really feel now in the sober light of day. If I'd taken advantage of you, because that's what it would have been, you might have regretted it later. We both might have."

Will took a breath. Jack was watching him, waiting with a calm expression, as if this were the sort of thing he talked about every day. Will was struck by the unusual blue gray color of his deep-set eyes. They were trained on him as Jack listened. Will got the sense, as he often did when Jack listened, that he was listening with every part of himself. He didn't fidget or fool with something on the table or in his hand, glancing from Will's face to something else of interest in the room, poised to interject his own thoughts or opinions at the first opportunity, as most people Will knew did.

Knowing Jack was listening, really listening, gave Will the courage to continue. "I guess I'm trying to say I think something could be happening between us, Jack. Something I've only dared fantasize about until now. Your coming here today gives me hope. Maybe that hope is misplaced, and if so please forgive me, because the last thing I want to do is make you uncomfortable.

"I've come to value our friendship in the short time we've known each other. It means more to me than a one-night stand. Way more."

He folded his hands on the table and tried to smile. "Okay. Your turn." The ball was in Jack's court. He waited to see if Jack would return it.

Jack nodded slowly, as if weighing his words before delivering them. He lifted his coffee mug and took a sip. He set down the mug and said, "I have to tell you, I've been thinking a good deal about what went on between us last night. You should know, since Emma died, I really haven't opened up to anyone the way I've opened up to you. I don't know why, exactly. I mean, I guess I was in mourning at first. We'd grown up together, me and Emma. She was what I knew.

"Then it just got so I was used to being alone. I've never been a very social guy. I mean, I like people, for the most part, but give me a good block of wood and a lathe and I'm happy as a clam, building something in my workshop. It was easier to hide, I guess. To let well-meaning friends drift away after I turned them away enough.

"Getting back to work was good for me. Not just financially," he grinned and continued, "but because it forced me back into the world. It required me to be sociable, or at least to communicate on a daily basis with some part of the human race. But still I didn't really connect with people. I mean, I'd talk to them, of course, but I certainly never made friends with anyone outside the confines of the workday.

"Then you came along, so interested in my work, so interested in"—he paused, flushing—"in me. I mean, at first I just took you at face value. I figured you really wanted to know about the history of tin ceilings in the area." Will started to protest that he really *was* interested in that but Jack silenced him with a raised hand.

"Hey, it's okay. You don't have to pretend with me. That's what I guess I'm trying to lead up to here, though it's taking me a while. I've been thinking about it a lot actually, ever since last night. I think what happened between us is this, and you correct me if I'm wrong."

Will leaned forward. This was it. Jack was going to say thanks but no thanks, in his kind, rambling, gracious way and Will would have no choice but to accept his decree. He forced himself to be calm and tried not to leap to conclusions.

"Last night you told me in so many words you..." He paused and gave a small, embarrassed laugh. "I'm sorry, I don't know the right words for this sort of thing when it's between guys, so just bear with me. I don't even know the words grownups use for this sort of thing. It's been so long since I was in circulation, if I ever was. So I'll just say it best I can. Last night you admitted you had a crush on me. And I tried to tell you back that I do too."

Will stared at him, his heart beginning a rapid, steady patter.

Jack looked embarrassed but tried again. "I mean I"—his voice lowered to nearly a whisper—"have a crush on you too."

Will felt laughter bubble up and threaten to spill out. He forced it down, aware Jack was very serious and also very embarrassed by what he was saying. The last thing he needed was for Will to laugh at him. It was hard, though, not to smile. His language was so quaint, so junior-high sweet. A *crush*? They shared a mutual *crush*? Was the next step to ask each other to go steady? Or taking it back another generation, who would wear whose pin?

Though younger by more than ten years, Will felt older than Jack at that moment, and more than a bit jaded. The crowd he ran with, or had run with until recently, would think nothing of picking up a stranger in a bar, taking him home for the night and then promptly forgetting him once he was out the door.

Friendship rarely entered the equation. What a lonely way to live. Even with Paul, whom he would call a friend if pressed, the only thing they really shared in common was their workout at the gym and the sex afterwards. They rarely talked about anything that mattered, certainly not their feelings toward one another.

In that regard this was all new to Will too, as was knowing how to proceed with a man who hadn't said he was gay or even bi, but simply that he had a *crush*.

Well, it was a start, wasn't it? At least he hadn't told Will he wanted nothing more to do with him. Nor had he delivered the tired, painful speech about being just friends.

So there was hope. A quote he'd read sometime back that had always stayed in his mind surfaced now. "If it were not for hopes, the heart would break." He touched his chest, now covered in a yellow T-shirt, and knew his heart was very much intact. He grinned widely at Jack and, unable to resist, said, "You've got a crush on me, Jack Crawford? Well, that's just *swell.*"

To hide his embarrassment, Jack took another cannoli and bit into the delicious confection. He noticed a smudge of dirt on Will's cheek and resisted the urge to reach over the table and wipe it off.

He honestly had no idea what would happen next. Were they now supposed to go upstairs and have sex? His mind recoiled at the idea, while his cock lifted its head, decidedly curious.

Curious. That must be what he was. He'd heard the phrase before—bi-curious. Will was watching him, the smile lingering on his face.

"You know, the game's coming on in a minute. I was going to watch it. Do you like baseball?" Will asked.

Jack was taken aback for a moment. Mentally he chided himself, realizing he just assumed gay men wouldn't like sports. What a bigoted idiot he was. Aloud he said, "Sure. Do you think the Mets have a chance this year?"

"You a Mets fan too?" Will snorted. "They always have a chance—and then they break our hearts."

"Yeah," Jack agreed, feeling suddenly a lot more comfortable.

"You can't have cannoli and coffee with baseball." Will laughed. "I'll get us a couple of beers." He took two bottles from the refrigerator and they moved into the living room, settling beside each other on the large, comfortable sofa that faced a huge flat-screen TV.

The game had just started and the Mets were at bat. They talked about the players for a while, discussing statistics and the Mets' chance for the World Series. Jack leaned back against the cushions, feeling happy but nervous as a teenager on his first date.

He took a long pull of his beer and glanced toward Will, whose eyes were on the screen. Jack examined Will's strong, handsome features and again wondered what in the world Will saw in him. Was it only the thrill of going after something he couldn't get? Now that he had Jack, whatever the hell that meant, would he lose interest?

What do I want to have happen? What do I expect?

Will glanced his way and their eyes locked. Jack felt his heartbeat quicken. He clenched his beer bottle and realized he was holding it so tight it might shatter. With a shaky hand he leaned forward and set it on the table.

Will copied his action, setting his own bottle down. Slowly he reached out a hand and touched Jack's thigh, unconsciously mimicking the gesture Luke had made so many years before.

Jack felt frozen in place. He looked down at Will's hand, noting the long, slender fingers. His skin was lightly tanned, the soft hairs on his arms a golden brown. His touch was solid, the fingers gently gripping Jack's thigh muscle. It felt like he was squeezing Jack's heart muscle too. He could barely catch his breath.

"You okay?" Will asked softly. "Is this okay?"

Jack swallowed and nodded. It was okay. They were grown men who could do what they liked. He wasn't eighteen any longer. It was time, finally, to be honest with himself.

Will moved his hand along Jack's denim-clad thigh toward his groin. Jack's heart threatened to burst through his rib cage. Will moved his hand back down Jack's thigh and scooted a little closer. "Hey, Jack. It's okay. I'm not going to rush you. Please, slow your breathing if you can. Nothing's going to happen between us you don't want to have happen. I promise."

Jack met his eyes and gave a weak grin, keenly aware of the sudden shift of power between them. For the first time in his adult life he wasn't in complete control of a situation. It felt very strange—both scary and exciting. Will's voice was calming, his touch gentle, and Jack knew instinctively he could trust him. He took a deep breath and released it, willing his heart to slow and his muscles to relax.

"Okay," he said quietly.

Will stroked his leg, his fingers curling down over Jack's inner thigh. Jack's cock was nudging hard against his fly and, unable to resist, he looked down at Will's crotch. The bulge was unmistakable. Again his heart began a rapid tattoo, ignoring his efforts to relax.

Will leaned forward, his face nearly touching Jack's. Jack turned away. Will kissed his cheek. "It's okay," he promised. He kissed Jack's cheek again. Jack's lips were tingling with anticipation, and before he could stop himself, he turned back toward Will.

Their lips met in a chaste press. Their eyes were open, each watching the other as they kissed. Jack could feel Will was trembling. It occurred to him Will might be as nervous as he was. Somehow this gave him courage. He closed his eyes and parted his lips.

Will's tongue gently slid over his lower lip and slipped between his teeth. Startled, Jack pulled back, his heart thudding so loud he could hear it. Will pulled back too, his green eyes blazing, the color high in his cheeks.

Though he was scared, he couldn't deny the desire roiling through his blood. Was he gay, was he merely curious, did it matter? He wanted to kiss Will, to taste those soft lips again. He could work through this fear—Will would keep him safe.

He closed his eyes again and leaned forward, silently offering his mouth again. Will whispered softly, "Jack," and again their lips met. Will touched the back of his head. His own hands were frozen at his sides.

Will's warm tongue again slid along his lips. Jack felt it enter his mouth. Will tasted like coffee and beer. He smelled wonderful, like shampoo and some kind of subtle citrusy cologne. Their tongues began to intertwine.

Oh my God, I'm kissing a man. I'm kissing a man. For a moment he tried to pull away, his fears almost getting the better of him.

Will gently but firmly pulled him closer. "It's okay," he whispered again. "We both want this. There's nothing wrong with it. It's good."

It was good. It felt good. It felt better than any kiss he'd ever shared. He wasn't kissing a *man*, he was kissing Will.

Finally Jack's thoughts were suspended, or at least drowned out by the roar of blood in his ears. He knew he didn't want the kiss to stop. It felt so good, so right, even better than the stolen kiss so long ago with a different man.

Back then he'd been way too young and unsure to know what he wanted or to have the courage to seize it. Now there was no reason to hold back. He wanted this. There was no longer any question or doubt.

Without realizing what he was doing, he found his arms lifting and wrapping themselves around Will. He pulled him closer, kissing him back with all the pent-up passion of years of repressed longing. He could feel Will's heart pounding against his own.

Time seemed to suspend itself as they explored each other's

mouths. Will's hand moved from Jack's head to his neck, slipping beneath his shirt.

He ran his hands over Will's back, feeling the strong, well-defined muscles through the thin cotton of his T-shirt. Finally Will moved, pulling away from Jack's mouth, trailing his lips down his chin and throat, his tongue touching the flesh. Jack fell back against the sofa and Will flopped back beside him.

Slowly Jack focused on the TV screen. He hadn't heard a word of the game during their extended kiss. Even now he could barely hear the announcer over the thump of his own heart.

"Well, would you look at that? The Mets just scored a grand slam." Will turned toward him with a broad grin. "Maybe this will be our lucky year, Jack. What do you think?"

Chapter Seven

"I'll get us some more beer. These aren't cold enough." Will took the half-empty bottles and went to the kitchen, leaving Jack to compose himself. He dumped the tepid beer into the sink and put the bottles in the recycle bin.

He touched his mouth with two fingers, marveling that the man in the other room had let him kiss him—had kissed him back with more than a little enthusiasm. Will's hand dropped to his crotch, where his erection still raged. He slipped his hand into his pants and adjusted himself to be more comfortable. His hand lingered a moment, wrapping around his shaft as he closed his eyes, reliving the kiss.

His mind flashed to Jack, naked on his bed, his ass offered for Will's plunder. He could almost feel the tight, velvet grip of his muscles as he eased himself inside the virgin passage...

I want him—bad.

If Jack had been another guy, one of the men he'd brought home over the years for a little action, Will wouldn't have hesitated in his next move. He'd have returned from the kitchen with his shirt off and his jeans unzipped. He'd have held out his hand to his potential lover and said, "Let's go upstairs."

He didn't dare do that with Jack. He found he didn't even want to—not yet. He wanted to take his time, not only for Jack, but for himself. Something was different here—different than any prior or potential relationship. For once he didn't want to get to the action as fast as possible. For once he wanted to savor the anticipation, not fixate solely on the prize of a hard, naked body in his bed.

What must Jack be going through now? A lifetime's notion of his sexual orientation teetering, perhaps already fallen, in the wake of that extraordinary kiss. How bright his eyes had been when they'd finally let each other go. His cock was clearly erect in his jeans, pointing like an arrow toward his hip. It had taken every ounce of willpower not to grab it through the denim.

Will opened the bottles and returned to the living room. Jack was sitting much as he'd left him, leaning back, his arms now extended along the top of the sofa, his eyes on the screen. As Will entered, Jack looked over and sat forward, reaching out for the bottle.

"Thanks," he said, and smiled.

Will settled in next to him. "What's the score?"

"Mets 10, Astros 6."

"Excellent." They drank their beers. Will felt his rock-hard erection ease a little. He put his feet up on the coffee table and tried to concentrate on what the announcers were saying. This was best. Give Jack a chance to process things, to stay in a comfort zone as far as the two of them were concerned.

He became aware of Jack's leg, which was bouncing up and down in a nervous, somewhat-annoying jiggle. Casually, Will put his hand on Jack's thigh. Jack's leg ceased its anxious tap. He looked over at Will. "Sorry. Guess I'm kind of nervous."

"It's okay." Will smiled back. He removed his hand and returned his attention to the game. A few moments later Jack's leg again began its nervous twitch, his foot tapping a steady beat against the floor.

Will glanced toward Jack, who, upon becoming aware of his

look, again stopped his nervous movement. “Sorry.”

“It’s okay.” Will floated an idea that popped into his head. “Hey, maybe you’d like a massage. That might relax you, or relax your body at any rate. I’m told I give a mean massage. Would you like one?”

“You don’t have to do that. I’m just a little edgy, is all. I’ll be fine.”

“No, I want to. I’ll tell you what. I have a TV in my bedroom too. Come upstairs and I’ll put the game on. You can lie down and watch while I rub your back a little.

“Don’t worry.” He had to laugh at Jack’s sudden panic-stricken look. “You can keep your pants on. No funny business, I promise. Remember, this is one hundred percent at your pace and comfort level. I wouldn’t want it any other way.”

Jack nodded and stood. “Okay. Lead the way.”

Will sat on the bed, watching Jack as he unbuttoned his shirt and laid it carefully over the back of a chair. His chest was massive—a strong, burly barrel chest with curling dark hair sprinkled with silver. The muscles in his arms and shoulders were bulging. Will drew in his breath, enthralled at the man’s raw masculinity. He honestly hadn’t realized how strong and well-built Jack was, his body until this moment hidden in loose denim work shirts.

He suppressed the intense urge to kneel at Jack’s feet and pull his pants down those strong, thickly muscled legs. He had to resist the fierce temptation to drag his underwear from his body and take his cock deep into his throat, not letting go until Jack begged for mercy. Will shook his head, forcing the vivid images from his mind.

Jack looked decidedly nervous as he approached the bed. “Uh, how should I be? How do you want me?”

Naked on your hands and knees. “Just lie on your stomach,

with your head at the end of the bed so you can see the TV." Will grabbed the remote and turned on the game. Jack lay down, his movements stiff and awkward. Will's heart melted with compassion, even as his cock rose with desire.

He scooted closer to massage those massive shoulders. The muscles were knotted with tension. Will realized a full-blown back massage would be necessary. "Your shoulder muscles are really tense. I'm going to straddle your back so I can get a good angle, okay? You just relax and focus on the game."

Jack gave a terse nod. Will had his work cut out for him. If the man held himself any stiffer he'd break in two. He climbed over Jack's legs and settled himself over him. First he smoothed Jack's skin to get him used to his touch. In a way it was like calming a wild animal. He didn't want to make any sudden moves that might scare his quarry away.

Jack remained stiff beneath him, his muscles bunched and knotted at his shoulders. Will concentrated at first on his lower back, massaging and kneading the muscles on either side of the spine. Slowly he worked his way up the broad, strong back. Jack's skin was smooth and supple beneath his fingers.

Jack lay very still, though his body no longer held its rigid posture. Will moved his way up to Jack's shoulders. He took his time, first kneading the flesh, then going deeper, penetrating the bunched muscle with strong fingers until Jack groaned.

He didn't stop until the muscles surrendered all of their tension. Jack sighed, the sound low and sensual in Will's ear. Resisting the urge to lie down against Jack's body and press his cock against his ass, he instead forced himself to focus on what he was doing.

As he worked the muscles, he could actually feel them ease and uncoil beneath his hands. He pressed harder, not giving up until Jack sank against the mattress, his body entirely limp.

Jack turned his head, no longer even pretending to watch the screen. Will leaned over to see his face. His eyes were closed, his lips slightly parted. His breathing had become slow and regular. Will realized he'd put his potential lover to sleep.

He grinned ruefully to himself. "I'm so exciting he falls asleep on me." Still, he knew it was a testament of Jack's comfort level with him, and that was perhaps more important than anything else at this point.

He returned to a sweeping touch with his palms, keeping a gentle pressure against Jack's skin. Jack's arms were lying loose at his sides. Will massaged first one and then the other, pulling them out and away from Jack's body as he did so. Jack remained limp, sinking into deeper sleep.

He touched Jack's sides, feeling the ribs with his fingers. Jack didn't move. Will was tempted to roll him over, to focus his attentions on less innocent areas of Jack's anatomy. He bet that would wake him up in a hurry. His cock stiffened at the prospect, even as his mind nixed the idea.

Instead Will continued to stroke and smooth Jack's back and sides, as he remembered his first sexual encounter with another man. Well, another boy really, as they'd both been fifteen at the time.

Justin Peterson was his lab partner in tenth grade physics class. Until they'd been assigned as partners Will hadn't really known Justin, except to nod toward him when passing in the hall. He'd heard rumors Justin was gay, as Justin, unlike himself at the time, didn't try to pass as straight. He gave off that particular effeminate vibe some gay guys cultivate and didn't seem to care if he got made fun of, which he did.

"I'm having trouble with the homework," Justin offered one day as the lab was ending. "Would you maybe like to come over and help me with it? We could have pizza after, if you want."

Will thought about it. Justin was very good-looking, in an almost girlish way, with long straight hair, big brown eyes and a slender build. If Will went home with him, would everyone assume he was gay too? Did he care? Was this, at last, the time to make his declaration to the world?

He hadn't yet told his parents or his older brother, John. He had never been put in a position to deny it, and had told himself he wouldn't deny it when the time came, but the question had never come up. Sometimes, feeling reckless and lonely, he wanted someone to confront him, to accuse him of being what he in fact was. But, perhaps because he was strong and fast and good in sports, and went with Tracey Baker to the dance when she asked him, people just assumed he was het. It was easier, especially in school, to let them think so.

Making the decision all at once and the consequences be damned, Will said, "Sure. That sounds like fun."

They studied in Justin's bedroom. Will felt important and competent as he explained the concepts Justin had trouble grasping. Justin seemed so intent on the homework Will had a sudden uneasy thought maybe Justin had had no intentions beyond what he'd said—homework and a pizza after.

Will found himself let down by this. Here he'd geared himself up for some crucial, first-time encounter—his virgin declaration to the world, or at least to one boy, that he was gay and proud of it—yet Justin seemed to show no interest in the matter.

This fear was soon put to rest, however, when Justin shyly asked Will if he'd like a back massage. Will understood this for the code it was and his heart began an anticipatory thud.

"Is anyone home?" he asked. Justin had let them into the luxurious Manhattan apartment with his own key.

"No. My parents won't be home for hours. My older sister is

away at college. Carmen, the maid, is gone for the day. We have the place to ourselves."

Absorbing this information, Will nodded. Justin smiled broadly. "Take off your shirt," he said. "I can massage you better if you do that." Will agreed and pulled his shirt over his head, tossing it to the floor.

He lay on Justin's bed and closed his eyes, feeling very brave and very scared at the same time. *Relax*, he told himself, *it's just a massage. Justin's probably as nervous as you are.*

Justin straddled Will's ass, much as Will was straddling Jack's now. He massaged Will's back for a while. Eventually his hands strayed down to Will's sides. Will laughed nervously and twisted beneath Justin. "Hey, that tickles."

"That's because you're not relaxed. Lie on your back. I'll massage your chest. That's very important if you're to relax fully." Justin spoke with confidence. He lifted himself off Will, waiting for him to comply. Though Will didn't entirely believe him, he rolled over. Why not?

Justin lowered himself again, now straddling Will's stomach, his ass resting against Will's crotch. Could he feel the erection Will knew he was sporting? If so, he gave no indication as he continued to rub Will's chest. It was kind of annoying, but Will was too focused on Justin's ass against his cock to take much notice.

After a few moments Justin slid down, now straddling his thighs. He dropped his hands to Will's stomach, lingering for a few seconds before moving to his intended target.

His eyes on Will's face, he slipped his hands beneath the waist of Will's jeans. He inserted his fingers beneath the elastic of Will's underwear. They made contact with the tip of Will's cock and Will closed his eyes, his heart now beating a thousand beats a minute, or so it seemed to him.

Justin slid off his legs and twisted his body to get a better angle. He pulled at the button on Will's jeans and unzipped the fly over his very erect cock. Boldly he pushed the white briefs down until Will's cock sprang free.

"I *knew* it," Justin crowed triumphantly. "I knew you were gay, despite the jock act for the rest of them."

Will didn't deny it. How could he deny it, with his cock hard and throbbing in Justin's hand? It only took a few strokes and he was near to orgasm. He'd never come in front of someone else, or by someone else's touch. It felt incredible—way better than his own furtive groping in the dark.

Then Justin did something that short-circuited his brain and flooded his senses with pleasure. He lowered his mouth over Will's shaft, his warm tongue licking around the crown and down the sides. Closing his lips, he drew back upward, the suction sending Will into spirals of convulsive pleasure.

He groaned, half-sitting as he spurted into Justin's mouth. Justin swallowed and continued to suck and lick Will's shaft until his cock softened and he pulled away. He fell back on the bed, his heart a steady thrum, endorphins flitting through his blood like a drug.

"That was your first time, wasn't it?" Justin lay on his stomach beside Will on the large bed, leaning up on his elbows. "I could tell, the way you came so fast."

Will flushed, embarrassed at his virginal status, though of course it was true. "Yeah," he admitted. "I've never been with a guy. Or a girl for that matter."

"So the front with Tracey was just that, huh? A beard to hide what you really are. Are you ashamed of what you are?" Justin's voice had taken on a bitter, accusatory tone. Will tucked his spent cock back into his pants and zipped them up.

He turned toward Justin and said honestly, "It wasn't a

front. I never pretended to be her boyfriend. I just went with her to a dance, is all. People just filled in the blanks. They made assumptions."

"And you let them."

"That's right." Will felt himself bristle. Who was this guy to tell him how to conduct himself? He of all people knew how hard it was to come out, even in so-called progressive New York City.

Justin flopped back on the bed and blew out his breath. He put his hands behind his head and stared at the ceiling. Will lay beside him, looking up as well. The ceiling had been painted to look like a night sky, complete with myriad constellations dotted in glow-in-the-dark silver on a midnight blue background.

"I shouldn't be so hard on you," Justin said, his eyes still trained on the ceiling. "I should just be grateful you came home with me. I've been wanting to ask you forever, but I was scared. I was pretty sure you were gay, but what if you weren't? Or what if you just didn't want to come over?"

He touched Will's bare chest with his fingertips. "I'll tell you a secret. I've never been with anyone else either. I've fantasized about it forever, but this is the first time for me too."

Surprised, Will blurted, "But the way you touched me—I mean, it sure felt like you knew what you were doing."

"I just did what I would have wanted someone to do to me. I've got the same equipment, you know."

Will laughed and Justin grinned, the tension of a moment before gone. Will was very curious to see Justin's cock. He'd seen pictures and video on the Internet. He'd even seen guys naked in the locker room at school. Except for his own, he'd never seen an erect cock up close and personal. He'd never touched one, felt its girth, tasted its soft, silky skin...

"Can I try?" he whispered.

"What? I couldn't hear you."

Clearing his throat, Will repeated, "Can I try? To—to touch you? To do what you did to me?"

Justin didn't have to be asked again. Quick as a flash he was out of his clothes. He lay back against the bed, sporting one of the largest cocks Will had ever seen, before or since.

With a gulp of trepidation, Will lowered his mouth over the fat, spongy head as he gripped the base of the thick shaft. It tasted salty, the skin surprisingly soft—soft as satin stretched over steel. He could feel a vein pulsing beneath his fingers as he stroked upward, his hand meeting his mouth.

Justin moaned and grabbed his head, pushing him down against his cock. Startled, Will pulled back, letting Justin's cock pop free.

"Please, please, please," Justin begged, his huge cock bobbing between them. Will lowered his head, licking down the shaft with his tongue before again taking the cock into his mouth.

He sucked it like a lollipop, his own cock rising in his underwear as Justin groaned and writhed beneath him. After a few minutes, Justin cried, "Jesus, I'm coming! I'm coming!" He spurted against Will's tongue, the jism gooey and slightly bitter. Unprepared, Will reared back, the rest of the ejaculate hitting his cheek and neck.

Justin lay still for a moment, except for the rise and fall of his thin, bare chest. Will wiped the ejaculate from his face and neck and, not knowing what else to do, wiped it on Justin's bedspread.

Still not moving, his eyes closed, Justin intoned dramatically, "William H. Spencer. I do believe I am in love."

Will smiled now at the recollection. Justin and he began a secret, torrid love affair. Well, a sex affair at any rate, one which was to set the standard for his later interactions. They talked very little, but met regularly at Justin's house for rapid and repeated oral sex. At school they were distant, merely polite. Ironically it was Justin, despite his earlier accusations that Will was ashamed of his orientation, who kept that distance.

One day, months into their relationship, he confessed he did it to keep Will. "I don't want you to have to choose, you see. If I let you keep your little het game going at school, I get to keep you all for myself."

They never progressed past oral sex and kissing, and just before sophomore year ended, Justin's father was transferred to California. Justin was permitted to finish out the year, but then he disappeared and though they promised to stay in contact, they soon lost touch.

Will had missed the sex sessions, but hadn't really missed Justin. No one had ever made enough of an impression on him for him to miss them when they'd gone. He wondered if this was a shortcoming on his part or on theirs.

Probably both. For whatever reason, he'd chosen men who wouldn't matter, who couldn't hurt him, whose leaving wouldn't faze him.

He slid from Jack's back and lay down beside him, putting an arm tenderly over his shoulders. What must it have been like—to be married for so many years and then to lose one's spouse? Did he miss her? Did he wake up aching for her, turning to find her on her side of the bed before he recalled she would never lie there again?

During all those years of marriage, had he ever had gay fantasies? Was it possible to "become" gay so late in life?

Will knew it wasn't so much a matter of becoming, but of

becoming aware. He thought of Paul's argument about the continuum of sexual desire. Where did Jack fall on that spectrum? Was he merely bi-curious? Once that curiosity had been satisfied, would he reject Will and what he had to offer? Would he come to long for the caress of a woman's hand? For the secret folds of a female body?

What the hell am I getting myself into?

Jack moaned and opened his eyes. "Hey," he said sleepily. "I guess I dozed off."

Will smiled. "I guess you did."

Jack smiled back. Slowly he lifted his hand. With his thick, blunt-tipped fingers he touched Will's cheek. He kept his eyes fixed on Will's, his expression nakedly vulnerable—part fear, part question, part tenderness.

Will felt a peculiar pull in his heart, like someone was reaching in and grabbing hold. He knew as Jack touched his face it was no longer a matter of getting into something. He was already in—deep.

Jack's eyes slowly closed again, his hand falling from Will's face as he slipped back into sleep, a half-smile on his lips. Will resisted the urge to wake him, to pull him close and never let him go.

The "crush", as Jack had quaintly called it, had been building for weeks now. He was beyond the point of being able to step back. For the first time in his thirty years on the planet, his heart was laid bare. He was vulnerable. He was at Jack's mercy. He was—oh God, say it wasn't so—in love.

Chapter Eight

Jack opened his eyes, squinting in the twilit room. For a moment he didn't know where he was. He knew he felt very comfortable, his body deeply relaxed against a firm mattress covered in soft bedding. He was on his stomach, his face toward the window, through which the sun was setting in extraordinary gold, pink and deep crimson red splashed over a darkening blue sky.

He could hear water running. As he came fully awake he recalled where he was, on whose bed he lay. The sound was the spray of a shower, Will's shower. He looked toward the bathroom. The door was ajar.

He sat up and ran his hands through his hair and indulged in a long, lingering, satisfying stretch. He hadn't felt this relaxed, this physically at ease, in as long as he could remember. He felt energized—ready to run a marathon or swim a mile in the ocean. He felt happy.

Swinging his legs over the bed, he looked around for his shirt and spied it where he'd left it on the chair in a corner of the room. He stood and moved toward it, his path taking him past the open bathroom door.

Unable to resist, he peeked inside. The room was warm and damp, billows of steam fogging the mirrors and swirling in the air. He stepped across the threshold before he realized what he was doing.

He froze in his tracks, riveted by the scene before him.

The shower was enclosed in glass, set into the corner of the room. Unlike most showers Jack was familiar with, this one's glass was clear. Through the droplets of water and steam he could see Will's bare body. He knew he should turn around and leave the bathroom at once. He was being impolite. He was spying.

Yet he didn't move, his eyes held by the sight, which was marred only by a thin veil of steam. Will stood with one hand pressed against the wall, the other wrapped around a long, thick cock. His head was back, the spray hitting his throat and chest.

Jack moved closer, compelled by some force stronger than he could fight. He watched the long, elegant fingers curled around the soapy shaft, gliding up and pulling down in a manner Jack knew well.

The movement was slow and sensual. Jack felt his own cock harden at the erotic sight of the naked man pleasuring himself. Hardly aware of what he was doing, Jack dropped his hand to his crotch, massaging his stiffening member through the denim as he stared at Will's erotic, graceful movements. Though he knew he should leave, he couldn't tear his eyes from Will's body, from his hand on his sex, from his lean, muscled torso, from his head, tilted back, the lips parted as if waiting for a kiss.

Jack cupped his erection, his balls tightening. He licked his lips and tried to swallow. *Get out, before he sees you.* He ignored the silent voice, barely audible over the beating of his heart.

Will's movements became more rapid, his chest beginning to heave, his mouth open as his hand flew over his cock in a frenzy. All at once Will stiffened and jerked forward with a small, stifled cry. He dropped his hands to his sides and moved so he was standing directly beneath the spray. Jack could see his cock through the steamy glass, still rigid, bobbing lewdly from his groin.

Face burning, heart pounding, Jack backed out of the bathroom, not sure if Will knew he had spied on him, praying he had not. He was stunned not only by what he'd witnessed, but by his own reaction to it.

Again he dropped his hand to his crotch. His cock was hard as bone. Unable to help himself, he massaged it through his pants, though he actively resisted the urge to slip his hand into his underwear.

Oh my God. I'm gay.

He shook his head. *No, no. You just appreciate physical beauty.* That must be what it was. Just as he appreciated the elegant curve of a fine piece of wood, Jack had always appreciated the human form, both male and female. It didn't make one gay just because one admired the curve of muscle, the lines and angles of something beautifully formed.

The image of Luke rose in his mind. Were his eyes really the same vibrant green as Will's, or was he confusing the two men along with his feelings? He sat heavily on the chair, his hand still on his cock. Luke had accused him of denying his feelings. At the time Jack had been too scared and confused to admit there was any truth to Luke's assertion.

As now, back then his body had responded honestly before he had a chance to shut it down. Over twenty years later he could still recall the power of that one kiss, the fierce, melted heat of his desire when Luke had grabbed his cock and stolen an orgasm.

Had he stolen it? Or had Jack, by barely resisting, by pretending to a confusion so great it rendered him helpless, been complicit in the act?

The kiss he'd shared with Will had been just as powerful, but sweeter, far sweeter. He had wanted that kiss, had actively sought it out. The fear he'd experienced at eighteen was still there at forty-four, but now there was also desire, a desire he wouldn't deny, not this time.

When Will had straddled his ass, his strong, capable hands massaging Jack's muscles into submission, he was glad Will couldn't see the erection sprouting beneath him. Will's touch left trails of electric desire over his skin, though once he began to massage Jack in earnest, his powerful, skilled touch had left Jack undone. His body had completely relaxed, unwinding from its constant vigil, though he no longer knew what he was guarding himself against.

What if, instead of falling asleep, he had twisted beneath Will and pulled him into his arms? Jack shook his head. As powerful as the image was, he knew he wasn't yet ready for such a bold act. Nor was he entirely sure how Will would react to such forwardness on his part.

Quickly he dropped his hand from his crotch as Will came into the bedroom, the lower half of his body wrapped in a towel. Jack shifted on the chair, crossing his legs to hide his lingering erection.

Will's hair was wet, his skin glowing. "Hey, you woke up. You were sleeping so soundly I hated to disturb you." Jack watched Will's face, looking for hints he'd known Jack was in the bathroom, but his expression was open and completely without guile. With enormous relief, Jack realized he'd escaped undetected.

Will walked toward him and for one crazy second Jack thought he was going to bend down and kiss him. He tensed, not sure how to react. But Will simply leaned over, reaching out toward the lamp that stood by the chair Jack sat in. He flipped it on, oblivious to Jack's sudden, hot blush.

"It's getting dark in here. Sun will be down soon. I don't know about you, but I'm starving. Can you stick around a while? Would you like to go out and get something to eat?"

Jack's stomach rumbled at the mention of food. He knew whether or not he was ready for something more with Will, he definitely wanted to "stick around". Sharing a meal would be a good way to ease himself back into a comfort zone.

"That'd be great. Did you have somewhere specific in mind?"

"I did, actually. There's this English pub I like to go to from time to time. They have good ales and dark beer on tap and hearty food. They have darts too. I'm quite a bit better at darts than at pool." He laughed. "Maybe I could challenge you to a game."

Jack grinned. "Sounds like the perfect evening. But am I dressed okay?" He glanced down, realizing he'd been so caught up in his thoughts he'd forgotten to put his shirt on.

"The jeans are fine. Would you like to borrow a shirt? I mean, you can wear the work shirt, of course, but if you wanted something different, I've got a whole closetful. Take your pick."

He moved toward the closet and slid back the doors to reveal several dozen button-down shirts. "This would look nice on you, I think. It's got a looser cut than most of my shirts, so it should fit your broader build okay." He held up a white shirt. Jack took it, surprised by how soft the material felt between his fingers.

He stood to put it on. Will watched as he buttoned it, making Jack self-conscious. "Does it look okay?"

"It looks great. Shows off your massive chest and shoulders. From this moment that shirt belongs to you. It looks like it was tailor-made for you."

"Oh, I couldn't take your shirt—" Jack began, both embarrassed and pleased by Will's praise.

"Take it. You can see I have more than I need, and that one never fit me right anyway. It would make me happy if you kept it. Then every time you wear it you can think of me."

They stood smiling at one another for several seconds. Suddenly Jack realized Will, wrapped in only a towel, must be waiting to get dressed. "I need to stretch my legs. I'll be downstairs." With a few long strides he reached the door.

Will pulled on black silk bikini underwear and black jeans. He decided on a black button-down silk shirt as a complement to Jack's white one. He hadn't been kidding when he'd said it looked tailor-made for him. A body like that shouldn't be hidden.

He picked up Jack's worn denim work shirt and looked at the tag. It was easily several sizes too large, even for Jack. Though he hated to admit it, the stereotype of straight men not knowing how to dress was all too often true. Jack's jeans were baggy too. He'd look hot with those thickly muscled thighs wrapped in form-fitting black denim or even better, leather. Will laughed to himself, doubting he'd ever get Jack in leather.

One step at a time, he told himself with a grin. One step at a time. He lifted Jack's shirt to his face and inhaled deeply, Jack's manly scent permeating the garment. It was part sweat, part something woodsy and fresh, part aftershave. He folded the shirt and gently placed it on the bed before returning to the bathroom to get ready.

Things were already progressing at a rate he'd never have dreamed of only a few days before. What a serious turn-on it had been to realize Jack was standing inside the bathroom door, rooted to the spot as he watched Will touch himself. He'd tried to draw out the show once he'd realized he had an audience, but knowing Jack was watching had excited him so much he couldn't hold off for long.

He'd decided as he dried off he wouldn't let on to Jack he'd seen him peeping. Knowing Jack the little he did, he figured it would be too embarrassing for him to admit at this point. Though he was dying to find out if Jack had been excited by his little show, or simply curious, he knew now wasn't the time to probe.

They'd go out to the pub and have a nice, uncomplicated, non-threatening time. Maybe he would invite Jack to come back home with him afterwards or maybe he wouldn't. Jack would let him know, one way or the other, the right thing to do. One step at a time...

Over hot, crispy fish 'n' chips and pints of Guinness Stout, Will and Jack talked about their work, about movies they'd seen, about politics, about the stock market and the price of gasoline, about everything except what was simmering just below the surface, at least for Jack.

He kept seeing the image of Will naked in the steam, his head thrown back, his shaft in his hand... Again his cock nudged for attention. Jack grinned to himself, thinking he hadn't had this many erections since his teenage days, when the slightest provocation sent the blood hurtling to his groin.

It was hard to follow the thread of whatever Will was talking about. Jack took a deep breath and let it out slowly. He forced himself to calm down and pay attention. He was going to have to stand up in a minute to play darts and the last thing he needed was a telltale erection bulging in his pants.

Will prattled on, his conversation completely devoid of even a hint of the sexual tension that had sprung up between them at Will's place. A part of him was relieved at this reprieve but at the same time he felt put out. Was that amazing kiss no big deal to Will? Did he kiss and then massage every guy he had to his house? Had Jack wildly misinterpreted the whole thing?

This was so new, this feeling of being out of his ken. Jack's life had always been so predictable, so easy, so—dull. He had spent a lifetime playing it safe. He didn't make waves. He did what was expected. He'd married Emma when told that was the proper thing to do. He'd put college on hold because a father supported his children.

He'd never experienced fireworks with Emma, though she had been a lovely woman. Part of it was because of her hesitation, even resistance to the act of sex. At first he tried to get Emma to see her naked body was beautiful, but he'd given up early on. Emma had been ashamed of her body, not because it was ugly, far from it, but because she'd grown up believing the human body was sinful and shameful and should be hidden. Sex was something to be engaged in furtively, always in the dark, for his pleasure perhaps, but not for hers.

The tone was set that very first night when they were still seniors in high school and she'd let him have his way. She had, he was to realize later, used the carrot of sex as a way to control him, to *win* and *keep* him. There had been no pleasure, only eyes squeezed shut and fists clenched as she'd urged him to hurry and finish.

Young, horny, stupid and still fleeing the feelings Luke had stirred in him, he'd mistakenly thought she was only frightened because it was the first time. He was frightened too, but too horny to care.

She'd been a *dutiful* wife, permitting him to have sex with her once or twice a week for the duration of their marriage, except during and just after pregnancy. To his knowledge she'd never had an orgasm. "It's okay," she would assure him. "I don't need that. This is for you. Just hold me. That's all I want."

At first he hadn't believed her. During the first year of their marriage he was convinced he could change her. He would be the one to help her tear down the stupid, misguided notions that had warped her thinking and inhibited her ability to receive physical pleasure. If he could get her to relax enough, he'd show her what she'd been missing. She would be grateful and become his secret sex goddess.

She'd punched him hard in the side of the head the first—and only—time he'd tried to lick her pussy. "That's disgusting! It's filthy!" she exhorted him, her face red with shame and anger. "Get away from me. Don't you ever do that again, Jack Crawford."

Nor did she ever touch his cock with her hands, and certainly not with her mouth. At least she had seemed to enjoy the missionary sex they had well enough. She would sigh and murmur to him she loved him, and squirm beneath him to help him come more quickly, but there had been little passion between them.

At first he blamed it on the pregnancy, which had preceded the marriage. They'd never had a chance to be carefree. After that he blamed it on the demands of young motherhood, then on the passage of time leaving her bored with him. After a while he put it out of his mind altogether. It was what it was, and she was a wonderful wife in every other respect.

Watching Will, who was smiling and gesturing animatedly, it occurred to Jack the lack of passion in their marriage hadn't been entirely Emma's fault. Perhaps he had been as mechanical and predictable as she, using her body as a receptacle for his lust, without examining his own complicity.

Perhaps he hadn't been meant to be with a woman.

The thought was too dangerous for the moment and he pushed it aside with a physical shrug of rejection. Yet, thinking back, he'd never experienced as powerful an orgasm with Emma as he had that one night with Luke.

Could it be he'd spent a lifetime living the wrong life?

You're as repressed and hung up as all the other assholes. Had Luke been right? Jack had vehemently denied it at the time. But then, the very nature of repression means you don't know you're doing it. You're hiding from yourself—from your very nature. He'd kept the cover intact for years—a lifetime. Yet now, with a single kiss, Jack found the very fabric of who he thought he was unraveling.

"You're not listening to a word I'm saying, are you?" Will accused, though he was smiling, his green eyes sparkling.

"What? No, I am. You were talking about how the stock market impacts the cost of fuel, or was it the other way around...?" Jack grinned and shrugged in defeat.

"That was twenty minutes ago." Will laughed. He stood and pushed back against his chair. "How about a game of darts? Loser buys the winner another round of Guinness."

"It's a deal, though I think I'll switch to Coke."

In darts they were much more evenly matched than at pool. They each won a game, then Will broke the tie in the ninth inning of the third game. They returned to the table, fresh drinks in hand. Jack felt considerably more relaxed, the physical activity of the game perhaps sublimating some of his lingering sexual energy.

Jack finally dared to turn the conversation toward what had happened earlier that day.

"That kiss—" he began. He felt his cheeks warming and

hoped the room was too dim for Will to notice. *...was amazing. Was the most incredible kiss I've ever experienced. Was the first time I've kissed a man...* No. He wasn't going to lie. In fact, maybe that was the key. Maybe, if he confided in Will, if he told *someone* what had happened over twenty years ago, he might be able to understand it better. To process it and see how or if it had anything to do with his reactions and desires now.

"That kiss," Will repeated softly, his expression gentle but coaxing.

"It—it wasn't my first time."

Will tilted his head, a question on his face. "Well, I wouldn't think so. I mean, you *were* married and all."

"No, no," Jack said, flustered. As he saw the smile slide over Will's face he realized he'd deliberately misunderstood. He was teasing him. How could he make light of something so monumental?

Maybe it wasn't so monumental? It was just a kiss. Jack was making it a huge deal, but was it? "A guy," he finally said. "I kissed a guy once. A long time ago. We were best friends. His name was Luke. We were just kids, barely eighteen." He held his breath as he waited for Will's reaction.

Will nodded, though he didn't seemed stunned by the revelation, far from it. "Well, okay. Lots of people experiment. It's perfectly normal. It doesn't mean you're gay."

"We did more than kiss." Jack knew his face was crimson now, but he was determined to make Will understand the import of what he was confessing. "At least—at least he did. To me." He hid his face behind his soda, draining the glass.

Will looked considerably more interested. "Is that right? But then you married..."

"Yes. The next night my girlfriend and I went all the way. She got pregnant. We got married. End of story."

"Wow. And this guy—"

"Luke."

"Luke. What happened to him?"

"He left town. Disappeared. He was my best friend since we were twelve but I never saw him after that."

"So it was just the one time."

"Yes."

Jack waited while Will digested this. After a moment Will smiled. "It's okay. That still doesn't make you gay."

Jack set down his glass rather too hard on the table. He realized he had wanted Will to confirm he *was* gay, or if not gay, at least curious. Bi-curious. He plunged on, saying what he'd never dared say to himself for so many years. "I liked it. Don't you see? I was so turned on. I've never experienced that level of intensity since, never. Never until," his voice ended in a whisper, "today."

Will was silent for several beats. "I don't know what to say."

"Was it—for you, was it something special too? I mean, am I just making a big thing out of nothing?" Jack heard the hint of desperation in his voice. He stopped, swallowed and cleared his throat. He was a grown man. He could be honest. Maybe for the first time in his life, he could be truly open with someone, no matter how scary it felt.

"I have to tell you, Will, I have no idea what I'm doing right now. I don't know the next step. I don't know what you see in me, *if* you really see anything in me beyond a little diversion. I'm way the hell out of my ken here. You have to know that. I guess I'm saying I need your help. I don't know the game we're playing now. I don't know the rules. I don't know how to play." Jack knew he sounded hopelessly naïve, but then he was, wasn't he?

That kiss, and the way Will had touched him afterward, his hands stroking his back, easing his muscles, luring him into sleep, only to awaken to see the sexy younger man, naked and taking his pleasure...

Jack felt raw, frightened, excited, almost timid and yet at the same time wildly energized by the realization his life had just exploded with possibility he'd never dreamed of until now.

Will was watching him, his gaze intense, almost fierce. "It's not a game, Jack. There are no rules. I know this is very new for you. I want to hear more about you and Luke. I want to understand better what your feelings are, and your expectations. Whatever this is between us, I want us to take our time. If it makes you feel better, this is all new for me too."

"What? But you—"

Will raised his hand and Jack pressed his lips together and waited. "I mean the feelings. Sure, I've been with guys. Lots of guys, which I'm not especially proud of. What I mean to say is I've never been in love." Now it was Will's turn to blush, which had the net effect of calming Jack down. "Not to say we're in love," Will hastened to amend.

"No, no of course not," Jack agreed.

"I guess what I mean is, this level of feeling, this depth of connection—I've never experienced that before. I'm a virgin, if you will"—he grinned, his expression suddenly impish—"in the ways of love."

The smile slid from his face as he said, his tone suddenly sad, "I've never had a committed relationship ever, with anyone. Until now that never bothered me. I think I took a kind of perverse pride in it, if you can believe that. I guess it kept me safe. It sounds so clichéd, I suppose, but if you don't fall in love, you can't fall out of it. If you don't put yourself out there, emotionally speaking, you won't get hurt.

"And it's worked great for me, if you don't count chronic loneliness masquerading as free-spiritedness. If you don't count waking up next to someone whose name you barely remember, or worse, fucking them and even during the act itself knowing you never want to see them again.

"They say timing is everything. Maybe it's true. I turned thirty and realized my life was for shit. I have money and a career that completely consumes my life, except for the time taken to have meaningless sex with virtual strangers or men I know I could never truly love. I leave it all to try and find some peace and *wham.* Enter Jack Crawford."

"A guy fourteen years your senior who has no earthly idea what he's doing at this point," Jack interjected with a rueful grin.

"So what? That's the point I'm trying to make, I guess. I have no idea either. I'm, to use your phrase, completely out of my ken as well. In uncharted waters. For you it's physical, for me it's emotional."

Jack pondered what Will had just said. It honestly hadn't occurred to him Will was experiencing an iota of the angst he had been consumed with these past few days. Though he still didn't know what he was supposed to do, how he was supposed to react, or what was in store for the two of them, knowing Will was, in some ways, as scared as he was, made it easier to contemplate.

He wanted to reach across the table and put his hand on Will's as a gesture of comfort, but years of conditioning prevented him from doing so in a public place. Instead he patted Will's arm.

"I guess we'll stumble through this together, then," he said.

"Okay then. Just, Jack, you have to promise me something." Will's expression was earnest.

Jack leaned forward, letting his own smile fade. “Yes, of course. What is it?”

“Be gentle with me. I’m a virgin.” Will kept his expression serious for a moment but then a smile curved his lips upward and he exploded with glee. Jack cuffed Will’s head.

In spite of himself, he laughed too, his heart lighter than it had been in years. “Let’s get out of here.”

Chapter Nine

"This is solid brass. You polish it up and you've got yourself a beauty." Jack stroked the side of the battered old telescope Will had retrieved from the attic. They were outside on his back deck, the telescope mounted on a tripod, its lens aimed toward the heavens.

Will watched Jack tinker with the knobs as he put his face to the eyepiece. It was a perfect night for stargazing, clear and warm, the moon not yet risen, but Will only had eyes for Jack. Though he knew he shouldn't read anything into Jack's words—after all, they'd both just agreed they would take it slow—when Jack had said, "Let's get out of here", Will's body had responded with conditioned desire.

In his lexicon and experience, the phrase was code for, "Let's go somewhere and fuck." Will, not used to sublimating his physical desires, forced himself to ignore the erection pressing like a bar of iron against his fly. He had promised to take this on Jack's terms, at his pace, and he had meant it.

Will had been with a few other bi-curious guys in the past, though more often than not he'd found their curiosity was more like uncontrolled, unbridled lust. After a few hesitant, perhaps awkward moments, they'd been as voracious and eager to get into his pants as any openly gay guy he'd been with.

Yet he knew with Jack it was different. His shy confession

about having once kissed a guy was at once endearing and arousing. It had been so long since Will had been with someone not intent on fucking him as quickly as possible, he barely knew how to act.

"Take a look at that." Jack stepped back from the telescope. "Just put your eye there, don't move the position. I've got it in perfect focus." As Will moved to obey, Jack stood just behind him. It took every ounce of willpower not to lean back against him. "That's Mars. Isn't that something? It's actually got a red cast to it."

Will peered through the eyepiece, focusing on the pale pink blob visible through the lens. "Can you see it?" Jack asked excitedly.

"Yeah, that's awesome," Will said, trying to inject some enthusiasm into his voice to match Jack's. Jack began to talk about polar icecaps and the atmosphere of Mars. Will stepped back from the scope and said with sincerity, "You really know a lot about astronomy."

"Me?" Jack looked embarrassed. "Not really. I've just read some stuff. I had these astronomy maps when I was a kid, plastered all over the walls and ceiling of my bedroom. My grandfather was a real enthusiast. He got me interested, I guess. It's just a hobby."

"Well, this old telescope hasn't been used in years. I'd be honored if you'd like to have it."

"Oh, I couldn't take that. That's a real antique. See there?" He pointed at some words ornately engraved in the brass. "This is a Dolland, probably from the early nineteenth century. That's mahogany on the barrel. The brass should clean up nicely. The lens is in excellent condition. This is definitely worth something."

"It's worth something if you use it. I don't know the first

thing about it. It would make me happy to give it to someone who appreciated it."

"How about this? I'll accept it, but I'll keep it here. That way I'll have an excuse to come out here whenever I want."

Will laughed. "You don't need an excuse, but all right. It's a deal." He wanted to go inside, to take Jack up to his bedroom and somehow get him naked. But how to do it without being too pushy?

Seizing the first thing that came into his head, he said, "You had mentioned some ideas about my master bathroom. Should we go have a look? I was thinking about that steam shower you suggested."

"Sure." Jack took the bait. "We can leave this in position and check out the moon later." He patted the telescope as if patting the head of a favored dog.

He followed Will into the house, through the kitchen and living room to the curving staircase. Jack turned back and gave the room a sweeping gaze. "This is a great old house. There's a lot of potential here."

"Yeah." Will laughed. "Potential. Not yet realized."

"Hey, the kitchen's done—that's a good start. That fireplace could use some work. It looks like someone tacked that faux marble mantel onto an existing one. Who knows what original work lies beneath it? Just look what we found under that hideous dropped ceiling."

"Yeah," Will said, wondering if he'd made a mistake in suggesting they look at the bathroom. Jack had seemed to switch to a business mode, his mind on renovation instead of his newfound *curiosity*. He would have to redirect Jack back to the matter at hand, he thought with a wry grin.

Standing in the bathroom, Jack seemed to lose his train of thought, his patter about possible designs for the space trailing off as he stared at the glass-enclosed shower. Will saw the color seep into his cheeks and knew he was recalling what he'd witnessed earlier that afternoon.

Will came up close behind him. "Did you like what you saw?" he said softly, his mouth close to Jack's ear.

Jack drew in a breath, his body stiffening. "I didn't mean to—"

"Hey, it's okay. I should have closed the door. Maybe I left it open on purpose. Maybe I wanted you to come in."

"Look, I—" Jack spun around, but whatever he'd been about to say, Will prevented by leaning down and kissing those wide, mobile lips. Jack started to pull back but Will stopped him by gently cupping the back of his head.

He moved closer so their chests were touching, Jack's heart hammering just below his. He stepped back and looked at him. Jack's eyes were bright, fear warring with desire in his expression.

"Your pace," Will whispered, taking another step back. "Let's go lie on the bed. I'll give you another massage. It'll help you relax." He turned and went into the bedroom without looking back to see if Jack followed. If he balked, if he said he had to go, Will would let him. Instinctively he knew whatever happened between them had to be on Jack's terms or not at all.

As he walked toward his bed he unbuttoned his shirt and let it fall from his shoulders. He kicked off his shoes and took off his socks. Time later to remove his pants—or not—depending on Jack.

He sat on the bed, only now allowing himself to see if Jack had followed him.

He had.

He stood at the foot of the bed. His eyes fixed on Will, he

slowly unbuttoned the shirt Will had given him. Will watched his large hands, noting the thick, blunt fingers. Though he knew from personal experience the claim hand size correlated to penis size was just an urban legend, he couldn't help but fantasize Jack's cock was proportionately as thick and long as his powerful fingers.

Jack dropped the shirt to the ground as Will had done. To Will's delighted shock, he proceeded to unbuckle his belt and open his jeans. His eyes still locked on Will's face, he slid the denim down his thighs and calves.

He was wearing dark blue cotton boxer shorts. Loose as they were, they couldn't quite hide the obvious erection poking against the fabric. Will's mouth actually watered and he had to swallow to keep from choking.

Responding to Jack's unspoken invitation, Will quickly stood, unzipped his own jeans and pulled them down and off. His black bikini underwear did little to hide his erection, the head of which was poking above the waistband.

Jack's gaze moved to Will's crotch. If anything, he got harder beneath Jack's intense, almost fierce gaze. Again Will sat on one side of the bed. "Come here." He patted the bed beside him. Jack stood frozen to the spot for several beats. Will waited, forcing himself to be patient.

Finally Jack walked around to the other side of the bed and sat awkwardly on the edge. "Come over here," Will said again. "Lie face down on your stomach." Jack obeyed, resting his head on folded arms, turning his face away from Will, as Will had expected he would. He reached over, stroking Jack's strong, bare back with his fingertips. Jack shivered to his touch but otherwise remained still. Only his rapid breathing gave away how he must be feeling.

Will scooted closer to him and brought his other hand over,

gently massaging Jack's massive shoulders, which had twisted themselves back into knots since the afternoon. "Hey, relax. It's just me. You know me. I'm not going to do anything you don't want me to do. Okay?"

Jack didn't answer. Will shifted, straddling Jack's lower back as he leaned forward to continue the massage. He pressed and kneaded the supple flesh for several minutes, pleased when it began to ease beneath his fingers. Moving lower, he worked on Jack's back by section, glad to note the deepening and slowing of his breathing as he relaxed into the bed.

Will began to smooth his sides, moving downward toward Jack's hips. He continued down until he was straddling Jack's calves. He focused on Jack's thighs for a while, massaging the thick, hard muscles. Ready to stop at the slightest resistance or protest, Will slid his fingers beneath the loose legs of Jack's shorts. Sliding his hands upward, he pressed his palms lightly against Jack's bare hips.

Jack had again begun to breathe rapidly, but otherwise he didn't move. Will kept his hands on Jack's hips for several moments, waiting for him to calm down. His hands still beneath the thin fabric of the boxers, cautiously he moved them up over the firm globes of Jack's ass. Jack stiffened, drawing in a quick breath. Again Will stilled until Jack relaxed beneath his touch.

Will had played this game before, but not for many years. After his first experience with Justin, he'd met Bryan during his freshman year in college. Bryan wasn't yet out but was definitely on the way. He'd invited Will back to his dorm room one evening and they'd given each other a massage.

Will had played it straight, not sure how far to go with Bryan, who, though he gave off decidedly gay vibes, liked to talk about his girlfriend back home. Bryan, however, when it was his turn to reciprocate, had done what Will was doing now, moving in baby steps from one forbidden area of Will's body to the next. Will had enjoyed the silent seduction.

He wondered if Jack was enjoying himself, or if he was too terrified to acknowledge the pleasure. Will's hands were firmly on his bare ass and so far he hadn't balked, leaped up screaming or tried to punch Will, so maybe he liked what was happening. Would he like what happened next?

Slowly Will moved one hand from Jack's ass and slid his fingers under his hip, using the give of the mattress to get where he wanted to go. He felt the silky touch of Jack's pubic hair. His fingers groped toward the thick, hard shaft pressed between Jack's body and the bed.

Trying to control his own rising lust, Will closed his fingers around Jack's cock. It was hot to the touch and stiff as steel. For several moments he simply held it. He could feel the pulse of Jack's heart thrumming in his shaft. How long it had been since anyone, male or female, had touched Jack so intimately?

Was it his imagination or had Jack shifted on the bed, his body slightly angled so it was easier for Will to grip his cock? Encouraged by this, Will slid his thumb up over the head of Jack's cock, finding the gooey drop of precome he'd been looking for. He slid his thumb back down along the silky flesh and repositioned his fingers. With his hand trapped beneath Jack's girth, he found it difficult to get a proper grip.

It was obvious Jack wanted this. His desire seemed to be greater than his fear. Taking a chance, Will leaned down and whispered, "Turn over onto your back. Keep your eyes closed. If you want me to stop at any time you just say that. Remember, your pace."

He let go of Jack's cock and moved off his legs to sit beside him. Jack didn't move. Then he rolled over onto his back, draping one arm over his face. Will was reminded of toddlers who think they can't be seen if they hide their own eyes. He grinned to himself. In a way Jack was a toddler, sexually speaking, though if Will had his way, he'd be growing up in a hurry.

He glanced down at Jack's groin. His cock was creating a little tent in his boxers. Will leaned over and lifted the elastic waistband to release Jack's cock from its cotton prison. He slid the shorts down Jack's thighs and tossed them off the bed.

"Ah," he couldn't help but sigh aloud. Jack's cock was as thick and long as he'd imagined, rising proudly from a luxurious nest of dark curls. "Jesus, Jack, you have a hot body."

Jack didn't respond. He might have been sleeping, save for the rapid rise and fall of his chest and the rigid shaft pointing upward. Will licked his palm and wrapped Jack's cock in his hand. He wanted to suck it—to impale himself on it—but he forced himself to slow down.

Carefully he moved his hand up and down the rigid cock, his other hand gently cupping the heavy, warm sac beneath. Jack groaned. Will's cock had snaked out of his bikini, half of it in plain sight, dark with blood and throbbing with desire. He could almost feel the tight clench of Jack's virgin ass around it. He closed his eyes and took a deep breath. Right now his focus was on Jack's pleasure.

Forgetting to go slow, he leaned down and closed his lips over the crown of Jack's cock. He tasted musky and warm, the very essence of masculinity. Greedily Will lowered his head, licking along the shaft, not stopping until he felt the head lodge in his throat.

"Jesus! Oh my God. Oh my God." Jack's voice came out a hoarse cry. Will stilled, waiting for Jack to tell him to stop. Instead Jack arched his hips ever so slightly, a silent cue to continue. His mouth still stuffed with cock, Will grinned.

He began to lick and suck Jack with all the considerable skill he possessed, using his hands to cradle and gently squeeze Jack's balls. Jack was groaning, his breathing rapid and shallow. Will licked in lazy circles down and then up the shaft before plunging onto it, not stopping until his nose met Jack's pubic bone. He held himself in this position until the need for oxygen forced him to pull back. Jack had begun to moan, a series of bleating, breathless cries.

After several minutes Jack gripped Will's hair with both hands, pulling hard as he again offered a cryptic prayer heavenward. "Oh, God. Please...please...God..."

Jack's balls tightened in Will's hand, his entire body suddenly rigid in the seconds before orgasm. When Jack shot his copious seed, Will was ready. Eagerly he swallowed, pulling back to lick every drop from Jack's shaft.

He lay his head on Jack's hip and reached up to touch his chest. Jack's skin was burning, his heart pounding so hard for a moment Will was worried he would have a heart attack.

"Shh," he whispered, "shh." He moved up beside Jack, who still had his arm slung over his face. His lips were parted and he was breathing hard. "Jack. You okay? You're kind of worrying me. Can you slow your breathing a little bit?"

Jack moved his arm and faced Will. His cheeks were flushed, his skin covered in a sheen of sweat, his eyes fever-bright. "I'm okay," he said in a hoarse whisper. "Better than okay." He pulled himself up so he was leaning against the pillows at the headboard.

Slowly he shook his head from side to side and let out a long, low whistle. "That was really something. That was a first for me. Now I know what the big deal is."

"You mean the first time another guy went down on you? I

thought you said you and that guy, Luke..."

"Not that. He didn't do that. I mean, what you did...with your mouth. No one's ever done that." Jack blushed and looked down, bringing his hands protectively over his spent cock.

"But surely Emma..."

"No." Jack shook his head firmly. "Not her. Never."

Will was silenced by this. He tried to imagine getting to the age of forty-four before having your first experience with oral sex. He failed. "Wow. No kidding."

"It was...amazing."

"Plenty more where that came from." He laughed. "And lots more besides."

Jack's attention was on Will's still-erect cock, half of it bared above the narrow band of black silk. "Can I...touch it?"

Will wasn't entirely sure he'd heard him correctly. "Can you touch it?"

Jack nodded. Will couldn't help but note the contrast of Jack's charming hesitation to the men he usually had sex with, who took what they wanted, no questions asked.

Will pulled his underwear off and tossed it away. He lay back against the pillows and put his hands beneath his head, closing his eyes to put Jack more at his ease. He felt the light touch of Jack's calloused fingers on his belly, then the grip of tentative fingers curling around his cock. He sighed with anticipation, almost desperate for Jack's touch.

Jack continued to hold his cock, his fingers cool against the heat of Will's lust. He arched up in encouragement but Jack remained immobile. Will opened his eyes and lifted his head a little to see what the problem was. Jack was staring at Will's body as if mesmerized, his lips parted, his tongue touching his lower lip.

"You okay?" Will asked.

Jack seemed to snap out of a daze. "What? Yeah." He dropped Will's cock and pulled away. "I'm—I'm sorry. This is so much to handle right now. I think I need some time. I don't know. To figure this out."

Ah, Will thought, trying to keep any bitterness from creeping into his thoughts. *Typical guy—now that he's come, now that he's had his orgasm, he's suddenly able to think clearly.* Was Jack now second-guessing himself? Regretting his haste in falling into bed with Will? Convenient that this happened *after* he'd let Will get him off.

Jack began to speak and Will struggled to listen without leaping to conclusions. "Please don't think I don't find you attractive. I *do.* I'm just—I don't know—I need to figure this out. The craziness whirling through my head right now. For you this is probably just an experiment. See how far you can get with the old guy—"

"No way," Will interrupted, suddenly angry. "I can't believe you'd say that. Do you think I've been making up everything I said? Do you really think I'd go to those lengths, say what I said about love, just to have a quick fuck with a virgin?"

"No, no, I guess not. Please, I'm sorry. That's just my insecurity talking. You're so good-looking and confident. I still haven't figured out what you see in me."

Mollified, Will replied, "Hey, I'm sorry I bit your head off. You don't know me that well. You don't know I never talk about touchy-feely things like love and emotion. I wasn't lying tonight when I said I'm as out of my ken as you are. Just in a different way."

"Maybe in a similar way." Jack looked down, his cheeks turning pink. "What just happened—it can't be just physical. I mean, can it? I've never experienced anything like that before,

Will. To tell you the truth, I used to wonder sometimes what the big deal was about sex. Why people, men especially, were so into it they'd do incredibly stupid things to get it." Jack lay back against the pillows and looked up at the ceiling.

"First the kiss this afternoon. I've been kissed before. I've even, as I confessed earlier, been kissed by a guy. But when *we* kissed it was different. It was like it was charged with something electric. No, not even electric—something cosmic. Something beyond my experience.

"And when you touched me this afternoon, sure it felt good. I mean, everyone likes a massage, but my cock was hard as a rock the whole time your hands were on me. And when I saw you in the shower..." He stole a sidelong glance at Will, who smiled and nodded for him to go on. "Well, when I saw you, so young and strong, your cock in your hand, your head thrown back... It was like I was watching a dance. The most sensual, erotic dance I've ever seen.

"Then just now. Oh my *God*. Your mouth, when it touched my cock, I thought I was going to explode. I felt like the blood was racing through my veins at a hundred miles an hour. It wasn't just that it felt good. It felt *incredibly* good. It felt like I had been waiting for your mouth to touch me like that my whole life, only I didn't know I was waiting. I've lived my entire life with a vague sense of discomfort, of being ill at ease in my own skin.

"Suddenly I don't feel that way. I feel like—" He paused and turned his head toward Will, his expression one of wonderment. "I feel like singing. I can't even carry a tune, but I feel like singing. I feel like dancing around the room. I feel like opening the window and screaming out to the world that my life is finally beginning." He took a breath and let it out. "I know this doesn't even make sense. You must think I'm insane. Shit, I think I'm insane. I was hoping by trying to say this crazy stuff out loud, it would make more sense. But it doesn't."

"Yes it does." Will was grinning so hard his cheeks hurt. "It does make sense, to me it does. I felt the same way when we kissed. And like you, I've kissed a guy before. A *lot* of guys." He touched Jack's arm and smiled reassuringly. "Jack, maybe you're over-thinking this stuff. It's partly my fault. I promised to go slow and then I couldn't keep my hands and my mouth to myself. I love how incredibly responsive you are. We have so much to explore together. Being with you is like the first time for me too, because I'm experiencing it through your senses in a way. Each touch, each feeling is new."

He took Jack into his arms. Jack leaned into him, hiding his face against Will's neck. Will's cock still ached with unrequited lust but he found to his surprise he wanted to put the needs of someone else before his own. He pushed the words whispering around the edges of his consciousness aside—*that's because you're in love.*

"Can you stay tonight? I would like it if you could stay. Maybe in the morning we can pick up where we left off."

"I'd like that. Only I don't want to wait until the morning."

Chapter Ten

For the first time that night, really for the first time since he'd begun to have sexual feelings toward Will, the unceasing, panicked patter in his brain stopped or at least quieted its incessant chant—*you're with a man, you're with a man, you might be gay, oh my God, you're with a man, you're touching a man, you want a man, you might be gay, you're gay, oh my God...* The anxiety was still there, but the terror was easing, replaced with a kind of wonderment. *You're with a* man—*with Will.*

Despite the fact he'd just orgasmed, his cock hardened as he leaned into Will's strong, naked body. His heart was still smashing in his chest and it was difficult to catch his breath. Will's cock pressed against his thigh.

When Will's lips had closed over his cock, pleasure had exploded through his body, drenching him in a soaking heat of sensation. How easily Will had taken him in, sucking his cock deep into his throat like it was the easiest thing in the world.

He had no idea what he was supposed to do next. Did Will expect him to suck his dick? Could he do that? Did he even want to? *I do want to, but he'd probably laugh me out of the room. I haven't the first clue what to do.*

He wasn't repelled by the thought of touching and sucking Will's cock. The realization was a strange one for a man who'd spent his life thinking he was straight as an arrow. No, he wasn't repelled, but he was scared. He'd spent the last twenty years with a sexually repressed woman, and instead of trying to help her grow, he'd simply capitulated, forcing himself to be content with what little physical intimacy they shared.

Now the world had split wide open. The sexy man at this moment kissing his neck no doubt expected him to return the favor he'd just bestowed. Unlike Emma, Will was anything but sexually repressed. He'd probably done things and had things done to him Jack hadn't even thought of yet. How strange it was to feel so young and untried, when he was fourteen years his lover's senior.

His *lover.*

Dare he use the word? Did the word imply love was involved? Or was it just a euphemism for a sex partner? Even that was a tough one to swallow. Jack tried to quiet his mind. Though Will had protested otherwise, this still might be just a kind of weird sexual experiment for him—an amusing diversion to see if he could seduce the handyman.

Well he had succeeded, hadn't he? Jack felt utterly vulnerable, completely exposed. He wanted to trust Will, and there was a fledgling trust balanced delicately in his heart for the younger man, but the slightest wrong move on either of their parts could send it tumbling, or so he thought.

Stop thinking.

"Hey," Will said softly, his voice low and sensual near Jack's ear. "Where did you go? I feel like you're off somewhere else right now. Come back to me."

Jack startled, surprised Will could sense this. He pulled away from Will's embrace and lay on his back, turning his head toward Will. "I'm sorry. You're right. I guess I'm lost in my own head. I still can't quite believe I'm here with you. I can't get a handle on what's going on between us."

Will leaned up on his elbow. A sweep of his hair fell in a wave over his forehead. His eyes glittered in the light of the moon now risen and shining through the window. "It's okay. We don't have to figure everything out right now. Whatever is going on between us, I like it. I hope you do too."

Jack didn't reply, unable to admit he didn't just *like* it, it was consuming him.

Will leaned down toward the bottom of the bed, where the sheets lay rumpled. He pulled them up over their naked bodies and lay back down. He closed his eyes. This gave Jack a chance to examine his face. The man was classically handsome, with his long, straight nose, square jaw, high cheekbones and smooth forehead. He was easily one of the best-looking men Jack had ever seen. Again he wondered what the hell Will wanted with him. Surely this guy could have his pick of any man he set his sights on.

He told himself not to look a gift horse in the mouth. For whatever reason, and for however long it lasted, at this precise moment, Will seemed to want him. And he wanted Will, oh yes he did.

Jack's gaze moved down Will's body. He could see his cock, still erect and outlined against the sheets. Tentatively he touched Will's chest. Unlike his own, it was smooth. His skin was cool to the touch, the muscle hard beneath it. Will was smiling, just a hint curving his lips. Gathering courage, Jack pressed his hand against Will's chest, feeling his heart tap a steady, strong rhythm beneath his fingers.

Holding his breath, Jack gripped the edge of the sheet between thumb and forefinger and dragged it down Will's body until his cock was exposed. It lay stiff and long, pointing upward along his stomach. Jack's cock was thicker, but Will's was longer, the head large and fat. Could he possibly take such a thing into his mouth?

Will opened his eyes and bit his lower lip, the gesture erotic. “That felt nice, when you touched my chest. You have such strong hands. I like the way they feel on my skin.”

Jack placed his palm over Will’s heart. He stroked his way downward, feeling the hard muscle beneath the skin. He felt dizzy, trepidation and desire churning in equal measure in his gut.

Will had let his eyes flutter shut again. Jack understood he was giving him space—giving him time to adjust to what was happening between them.

Jack moved his fingers down to Will’s stomach until they were a fraction of an inch from his cock. Unable to resist, Jack touched the head with one finger. Will’s cock twitched in response and he moaned.

Jack’s own cock had fully recovered. The scale of his emotions tipped between nerves and desire, desire winning out. He gripped Will’s shaft. It was hot to the touch, a thick vein pulsing up the side. Will’s cock stiffened beneath his fingers. He didn’t dare look at Will’s face, focusing instead below the waist.

Shifting downward on the bed, he moved his face closer to Will’s crotch. He could feel his own heart thudding against his ribs. He moved closer still, so his nose was almost touching Will’s cock. He breathed in, aroused by the musky scent.

Dropping his hand, he tentatively snaked out his tongue and licked along the smooth flesh. Again Will’s cock twitched at the touch, though he was otherwise still. Cautiously Jack licked upward toward the spongy head, drawing a circle around it with his tongue.

He moved to get a better angle, closed his eyes and opened his mouth. Slowly, his heart squeezing so tight he could barely breathe, he lowered his mouth over the bulbous head. He leaned down a little, trying to take it deeper. It already filled his mouth and he had managed barely more than the head. His heart was beating so hard he felt dizzy.

Will touched the back of his head. “Yes,” Will whispered, holding onto the “s” as he pressed gently against Jack’s hair. More of the shaft slipped into his mouth. Its head touched his soft palate and Jack gagged, not expecting it. Instinctively he jerked back and Will’s hand fell away.

Gasping, Jack thought, *I can’t do this.* He wanted to do it. He wanted to give Will the incredible pleasure he’d given him, but he knew he didn’t have the skill. Still, he tried again, lowering his head, his lips sucking down the shaft as he tried to imitate Will’s actions.

Again the head touched his soft palate and again he gagged, unable to control the reflex. *Shit.* He closed his eyes, waiting for Will to jerk away with disgusted impatience.

You can do this. Just don’t think about it. That didn’t work—this time he gagged almost the moment he wrapped his lips around the head. He was angry with himself and acutely embarrassed.

“Hey,” Will said, his voice tender. “Relax.” Humiliated, Jack looked up at Will. “I can see from your face you’re beating yourself up right now. Please don’t. This isn’t a contest. We’ve got plenty of time. As much time as we need.”

Jack nodded, still embarrassed but grateful for Will’s gracious reprieve. “What you did felt great,” Will continued. “You’ll be a natural once you relax.” As he spoke, he wrapped his hand around his own shaft. Jack’s eye was drawn toward it. Will’s hands were narrow, the fingers long and elegant compared to his own beefy ones.

Will curled his fingers around his cock, his thumb pressing

along the pulsing vein. "When I was in the shower," Will whispered throatily, "I was thinking of you. I was thinking about how much I wanted you."

Jack was unable to pull his gaze away as Will began to masturbate in front of him. Using his left hand, he gripped the base of his cock tightly as the right hand continued to stroke and pull at his shaft.

Jack's cock sprang to rock-hard attention. Will's green-eyed gaze was fiery, his tongue peeking between his lips, his chest rising and falling with each hot, sensual stroke of his hand.

Something in the gesture shot straight past Jack's whirling mind, heading right for his cock. Before he realized what he was doing, he pushed Will's left hand away, taking the hot, heavy balls below into his hand. Will groaned and let his head fall back, his right hand flying over his shaft.

Within a few moments Jack felt Will's balls tighten, as Will stiffened and gave a cry. He jerked spasmodically, shooting jets of cream onto his belly and chest.

His hand dropped away from his cock and, reluctantly, Jack also let go of his balls. Will opened his eyes and grinned weakly at Jack. "That just kind of snuck up on me. That was really hot."

Jack smiled back uncertainly. He was still wildly aroused, his cock jutting stiffly toward Will. *Hot* was an understatement. It was incendiary, combustive, molten.

Jack knew he was ready for Will to take him to the next step, whatever that might be. His cock ached to feel again the fiery perfection of Will's lips and tongue, which had driven him nearly insane with pleasure.

Will reached for the box of tissues beside his bed, wiping away the evidence of his orgasm. "You like to watch, huh?" he said teasingly.

Jack felt his face heat but he didn't deny it. Will held out his arms and Jack lay beside him. Will turned into him, resting his head on Jack's chest. "Your heart is beating so fast," Will whispered.

Will began to kiss Jack's chest—butterfly kisses that sent shivers of pleasure running down his spine. He stopped at Jack's left nipple and licked in a lazy circle around it, causing it to perk to attention. Lightly he bit the nubbin, sending electric currents of desire straight to his cock. He did the same with his other nipple and then began a slow, sensual glide down his abs and stomach.

Jack's cock ached in anticipation. Will gripped his thigh with one hand. The other hand gently closed around the base of his cock. Jack gasped, his heart lurching as Will's lips closed over the crown of his shaft. Will continued to lower his head, his lips creating a heavenly suction.

"Jesus," Jack moaned softly, barely aware he had spoken. Will began to move his mouth, lifting and lowering, his tongue dancing along the underside of Jack's cock while his lips did their magic, his fingers gripping the balls beneath.

Jack could feel an orgasm building. He gasped, the pleasure overwhelming his senses. All at once Will pulled away, letting Jack's cock fall wetly against his belly. Jack groaned, desperate for his touch, still too shy to demand it.

Will didn't keep him waiting too long, however. He bent again over Jack's cock and licked in a slow, teasing circle around the head, gliding over the slit, outlining the base of the crown with the tip of his tongue. Nearly overcome with lust, Jack grabbed his head and pulled him down, aware he was being aggressive, not able to help himself.

Will didn't resist, taking Jack's shaft deep into his throat. Will's finger prodded and teased between his ass cheeks. Jack stiffened, embarrassed and unsure about this sudden, if gentle invasion of his most private place. The finger was wet and pressed easily past the sentinel of muscle ringing the entrance. Though he was embarrassed, it felt good. He couldn't deny it. It felt great.

It was as if there were a furnace boiling deep in his belly—he was literally on fire. Whether in spite of or because of Will's intimate probing, Jack's climax welled up like an earthquake shaking inside of him, shattering through him, utterly beyond his control.

For an indeterminate amount of time Jack lay in a stupor, only barely conscious of the man beside him. Dimly he became aware of a harsh, rasping sound, which he eventually placed as his own ragged breathing. He realized his fingers were entwined in Will's hair, probably hurting him. He forced his cramped fingers to let go and his hands fell limply to his sides.

Will stretched out beside him. He leaned over and kissed him on the forehead, on his eyelids, on each cheek and finally on his lips. "You liked that, huh?" he said, the teasing lilt back in his voice.

Jack turned toward him, trying to focus. "Yeah," he said, a grin lifting the corners of his mouth. "You could say that."

Will laughed, happiness suffusing his features. Silently Jack marveled to think he was the source of this happiness in some way. He laughed back out of sheer joy and impulsively caught Will in a bear hug.

They lay together in post-orgasmic contentment, stroking each other's bodies and faces. They whispered back and forth, mostly the sweet romantic nonsense shared between new lovers. Jack felt sleep tugging at him but he resisted, wanting to savor this quiet, shiny new joy—a joy he'd never experienced before, a joy he hadn't known existed.

Eventually they quieted, content just to hold each other. Jack drifted on the edge of consciousness, sometimes wondering if this was a dream. If it was, it was the best dream he had ever had. He succumbed to Morpheus' lure, falling into a deep, peaceful slumber in the arms of his lover.

Sometime much later Jack awoke, drifting upward into consciousness, aware he was happy before he remembered why. The reason for his happiness was beside him. Will lay on his side, curled against Jack, his head resting on Jack's chest.

Jack stroked Will's hair. He looked out at the silvered moon, recalling the song about the lonely man who falls in love and then the blue moon turns to gold.

He didn't dare assign whatever was happening between them with the label of love, but this was definitely more than experimenting, of that he was certain. Yes, the sex had been *amazing*, but whatever was developing between them went beyond sex. A real friendship was blossoming, along with trust.

Jack, frightened but eager, had trusted Will, and that trust had not been misplaced. He marveled at how someone so young could be so wise and good. Not for the first time, he felt as if he were the younger of the two. In some ways, he supposed, that was true.

Will stirred and sighed softly in his sleep. Jack shifted and Will rolled away from him, falling to his back. He looked even younger in sleep, his lashes shadowing his cheek, his lips rosy and pouting.

Jack's mouth was dry. He also, he realized, needed to pee. Carefully he eased himself from beneath Will's sleeping form. He adjusted the sheet over Will's body, affection for the moment outweighing lust.

He went into the bathroom, flicking on the light. He used the toilet and washed his face. As he dried his face with a towel, he glanced at himself in the mirror and shook his head. No one he knew in the world would believe where he was right now, or what he had just done with another man. He hardly believed it himself. Time later, he thought, to figure it all out. Right now he just wanted something to drink. Will probably had water or juice in his fancy new refrigerator.

Quietly he moved around the room, finding and pulling on his boxers and jeans. He didn't bother with his shirt, or rather, Will's shirt. Instead he folded it and placed it, along with his belt, on a chair. With a last look at the still-sleeping Will, Jack left the room and went downstairs, heading toward the kitchen. He retrieved a bottle of cold water from the refrigerator.

As he drank it, he suddenly remembered the telescope, still set up on the back deck. He would bring it inside before the morning dew covered it.

Stepping outside in his bare feet, he breathed in the fresh spring air and looked up at the sky. The night was silent, save for crickets and the gentle rustle of the wind in the trees. It must be well past midnight, he thought. The stars had faded, outshone by the brilliant moon. He glanced at the telescope, smiling as he recalled Will's generous gesture in offering it to him.

He would take it safely inside, and then go back upstairs in a moment. But for now he savored the quiet peace, letting his mind fill with the strange wonderment of what had happened between them.

He sank into a deck chair and closed his eyes, leaning his head back as he recalled Will's incredibly erotic touch. He hadn't known such sensual pleasure existed. Even now he could almost feel Will's warm, wet tongue gliding down his shaft, sending spirals of heated ecstasy eddying through his cock and radiating out all the way to his fingers and toes.

Yet what they'd shared had gone beyond sex, as exciting as it had been. There had been a tenderness between them, a kindredness as Will had said, that surpassed mere physical pleasure. Jack was both excited and terrified by this realization.

"Will," he said aloud, "could it be I'm falling in love?"

Will woke with a start, immediately aware the bed beside him was empty. "Jack," he called. Maybe he was only in the bathroom. But no one answered. Will sat up, surprised at his strong reaction to finding Jack gone.

Usually he couldn't wait to get rid of a guy, once he'd taken what he wanted from him. With Jack, however, the opposite was true. He'd felt so happy just lying beside him, listening to the slow, steady beat of Jack's heart beneath his ear as they talked and whispered together. He hadn't even been aware of falling asleep.

He'd felt safe. Yes. That was the word—safe, in Jack's arms.

But where was he? Will swung his legs over the side of the bed and hurried over to his bureau, grabbing a pair of cotton pajama pants from the drawer. He poked his head in the bathroom just to be sure, but Jack wasn't there.

"Jack?" he called, as he hurried downstairs. Surely Jack wouldn't have left? Not without saying goodbye? "*Jack*," he said again, louder. He made his way to the kitchen and noticed the back door was ajar.

He stepped outside and saw him then, sitting on a chair beside the beat-up old telescope, his head back, his hands laced over his chest. "There you are. I thought maybe you'd flown the coop." He tried to keep his tone light, not wanting to admit how much it mattered to him that he had not.

Jack sat up and smiled at him. "I'm sorry. I didn't want to wake you. I just came down for a bottle of water. The air is so fresh out here. I was just enjoying it for a minute." He stood and they moved together into each other's arms.

Will lowered his head, bringing his lips to Jack's. They kissed for a long moment. Will could feel Jack's cock rising against his thigh. His own cock responded in kind.

"Want to go back upstairs?" he whispered.

"I thought you'd never ask," Jack said, his eyes sparkling in the light of the moon.

Chapter Eleven

"Yeah, I have to go. I have to pick up a shipment of lumber for a client. I'm going to build a deck."

"You work on Saturdays too, huh?"

"When you own your own business, you work whenever you can."

They were sitting at Will's breakfast table, sipping coffee and eating blueberry muffins. They'd returned to bed a little before dawn, again kissing, snuggling and exploring each other's bodies. They'd slept late into the morning, but since it was still the weekend and markets were closed, it didn't really matter.

It was a novel experience, taking his time with someone. Will loved Jack's newness. The way Jack trembled when Will touched his cock, a shiver of pleasure running through his body. He loved Jack's shy hesitation until pure lust left him raw with desire, eager for Will's touch.

He'd stiffened each time Will had probed his ass. Will knew Jack wasn't ready to go further than they'd gone—not yet. Hell, it was amazing he'd come this far, this fast, when Will thought about it. He wouldn't have minded taking Jack back to bed for the rest of the day to continue their sensual, slow exploration of one another.

Jack, clearly, had other ideas. He pushed back his chair

and stood. "Well, I guess I'll see you around."

Will was taken aback by this abrupt and less than warm goodbye. Hadn't they just spent the night together, wrapped in each other's arms? Maybe Jack was having second thoughts. Maybe he'd tried out the "gay" thing and was ready to move on.

Will's defenses went up almost before he could stop them. If Jack wanted to act as if nothing had happened—fine. Two could play at that game.

"Great," he said, his voice light as he forced a smile to his face. "I'm busy in the morning, but by afternoon I should be winding down."

Shit. Why had he said that? Now that meant Jack definitely wouldn't come back tonight. No, maybe that was a good thing. Let Jack sort through whatever weird stuff was going on in his head right now. The last thing Will needed was to babysit him through another bout of heterosexual angst. If he wanted to come back—well and good. If not, *c'est la vie.*

"Okay," Jack said. "Maybe I could stop by tomorrow evening. I'll give you a call before I come. If that's convenient for you."

Convenient? What had just happened? Where did the incredible sweetness and intensity they'd shared disappear to? Why was Jack's expression so closed? His demeanor so guarded?

Unable to get past what was probably just a defensive posture on Jack's part, Will felt himself stiffening in turn. "Sounds like a plan," he said, watching helplessly as Jack turned away.

Jack drove slowly along the road, his mind lost in thought. He wasn't sure exactly what had gone down but he knew he was largely responsible for it. Why had he lied about a job? He had no wood to pick up or deliver. He had no deck job.

He'd been watching Will eat a muffin, licking a crumb from his fingertip. The gesture had somehow struck Jack as intensely erotic. He had forced himself to remain in his chair, casually sipping his coffee, instead of leaping across the table to grab Will's hand and suck the finger he'd just had in his mouth.

He felt raw and incredibly vulnerable. Every nerve ending was alive and screaming from the amazing night they'd shared. It was the first time in his life he'd experienced such intensity. Beyond the sexual aspect, beyond the incredible physical pleasure, was something deeper, and much more frightening.

Jack Crawford was falling in love.

And the thought scared the living shit out of him.

Here he was, a forty-four-year-old widower with two grown sons. Sons who would be shocked, maybe even horrified, to discover their dear old dad was a queer.

Was he?

Am I gay?

When Will kissed him, he responded. Not just with his mouth, but with every fiber of his being. He came alive beneath Will's touch. His cock raged, throbbing and aching for Will's caress. Was it just Will, per se? Or did he love men instead of women? Well, in addition to women. He'd loved Emma. He'd been sexually aroused by her. How else could he have had sex with her for so many years? He'd never been turned off by her, or by any woman. He liked to look at pictures of naked women in the girly magazines as much as the next guy.

But this was different.

What was different, exactly? What was it that made this so much more intense? It wasn't just the newness of it. It wasn't just the novelty of touching and being touched by another man in such an intimate way. It was the *emotional* connection. That's what was different.

Is that, he wondered, *what truly defines our sexual orientation? Whom we connect with emotionally?* Though it seemed almost disloyal to Emma to admit it, he felt more of an emotional connection to Will than he ever had with her. Thinking back over the long years, he'd never felt so connected to someone, except maybe Luke...another man...

These thoughts and feelings, though not as well articulated at the time, had assailed him this morning as Will and he sat down together at the table. What in God's name was he doing, falling in love like a teenager? Because, while he knew Will was having fun now, there was no way Will could ever love him back. Oh, he might think he was in love for a week or even a month. But if Will's past love life was any indication, the thrill might quickly fade. He had admitted in several of their long, intimate conversations about their lives that he had never had a committed, sustained relationship with anyone, male or female.

Why should Jack have any reason to believe this time was different? Jack knew he shouldn't fool himself. He was nothing special. He wasn't particularly good-looking. He wasn't young. He certainly wasn't rich. No, the only thing he could offer Will at this point was the kick Will might get from initiating a novice lover in the ways of homoerotic play.

What a funny story to tell his buddies at the gym, to whisper to a young lover as they laughed in bed together. The thought sickened Jack. Sitting at the table with Will he had felt himself becoming defensive and angry, even though he knew he was only reacting to his own crazy, tortured thoughts.

Thus he made up the story about a job, as a way to save face for them both. He would make a graceful escape before Will had the chance to send him away.

Yet he hadn't shut the door all the way, had he? He'd said he'd be able to see Will tomorrow, after he finished his nonexistent job for the day. Even if this meant little or nothing to Will, Jack found he couldn't let it go—not yet.

At least Will hadn't said he was busy. Jack even fancied he saw a look of confused pain flash over Will's face when he'd said he had to get going. Maybe all of this really was just in Jack's head. Maybe he was being totally unfair.

Maybe, but he doubted it. Will could have said something, anything, to indicate he didn't want Jack to go. He hadn't said, *What about tonight? Why don't you come back later?* No, he'd gone blithely along, probably glad to get Jack out of his hair.

Fine. Jack Crawford forced himself on no one. The very idea was anathema to him. He clutched the steering wheel and pressed down hard on the gas. Usually a very cautious driver, he drove through an intersection just as the light turned red, feeling reckless, frustrated, confused and scared.

To make matters worse, his body recalled the hot, romantic moments shared together in the dark and his cock sprang up, aching for the man he was speeding away from. He dropped his hand to his crotch and massaged his erection through the denim.

Who the hell am I fooling? I want him. I want him in the worst way. I've never wanted anyone so much. Even if he's just using me, or keeping me around for his amusement, I am hopelessly, head over heels crazy for the guy.

He pulled into his driveway, parked and cut the engine. He sat still, lowering his forehead to the steering wheel. "Love," he said aloud, "is making a fool of me."

✧

The next afternoon the doorbell rang. Will, immersed in his work, didn't register it at first. When it rang a second time he realized what he was hearing. *Jack*. Was he here? He had said he'd call first.

Will hurried toward the front door, but instead of Jack, Paul stood on the other side, breathing hard, sweat beading on his forehead. He was wearing running shorts and a sleeveless T-shirt that accentuated his lean, curving muscles. He looked good enough to eat.

"Hey, handsome. I was out jogging and thought I'd swing by."

Will stepped back and Paul came into his house. "No handyman here today, huh?" he said with a grin. Will didn't answer.

Despite himself, he couldn't help but be attracted as he always was to Paul's sexy body, the dark skin glistening with sweat, his teeth white and straight as he flashed a smile in Will's direction. "Got a glass of water for a thirsty man?" he asked, wiping his forehead with the back of his hand.

"Sure, come on back." Will preceded Paul to the kitchen. He handed him a cold bottle of water and leaned back against the counter, watching him drink it.

What was Paul doing here? Usually they met at the gym, worked out and then retired to one or the other's place for sex. Will found himself a little out of sorts to have Paul just show up as he had. What if Jack also chose this moment to stop by?

Though he wasn't precisely hiding the fact of Jack's existence in his life, he wasn't yet ready to share the details, especially not with Paul. Until he was sure in his own mind what it was he and Jack had, he wasn't about to open it up to Paul's scrutiny.

Still, Jack had said he would call first, so he'd have time to shoo Paul away before things got awkward.

"You're quiet today. You seem distracted," Paul said. "Guess I threw you off, just showing up, eh?"

"What? Oh, no, that's okay," Will lied. "I just finished what I was working on. It's no problem." He paused, adding, "I am expecting a call in a bit..."

Paul raised his eyebrows. "Why do I get the feeling this call involves another guy? No secrets between us, right? It's not like we're lovers, heaven forbid. Maybe we can have a little three-way fun. Come on, out with it."

"No, nothing like that." Will bit his lower lip and turned away. Now why had he denied it? Did a part of him know whatever Jack and he had shared had been a one-time thing? Should he admit to himself Jack wasn't going to call—not tonight, not ever?

Paul looked unconvinced, but didn't press it. Instead he said, "Well, I'm going to finish my run. I've got plans tonight of my own." It was Will's turn to raise his eyebrows. Paul laughed. "What did you think? That I wait at home for you to say let's go work out and fuck? You know better than that." When Will didn't respond, Paul continued, "I met the hottest guy the other night at the gym. His name is Francois Laurent. He's French, recently transferred by his company. He's sexy as sin. He's taking me out tonight to Torch. I might be able to swing you an invitation, if you want to come along."

Torch was an exclusive gay club in the city, privately owned and known for the impromptu orgies that often took place in a room designed for the purpose, covered from wall to wall in mattresses and pillows, silver bowls filled with condoms and tubes of lubricant set discreetly about the room. Will had been to the club before. It had a waiting list a mile long unless you knew someone. He'd never participated in the orgies, though he knew Paul had.

"No thanks," he said with a laugh. "I've got plans already." *I hope.*

He walked Paul to the front door and opened it. "Hey, have fun tonight. I know you will." It was odd to admit he didn't feel even the slightest bit jealous of Paul's plans or the new guy he was with. While the sex had always been hot, there had never been more than that.

As they stood at the open door, Paul reached out unexpectedly and grabbed Will, locking him in an embrace. Before Will realized what Paul was doing, he kissed him hard on the mouth, only letting go when Will pulled away.

Paul gave him a smoldering gaze and then laughed. "Don't be a stranger."

As Will watched Paul jog down the road, he caught the back end of a red pickup truck as it drove slowly by. Jack drove a red pickup truck. Will stepped out into the yard but the truck had disappeared around the corner.

"Fuck. Fuck, fuck, fuck." Jack punctuated each curse with a bang of his fist to the steering wheel. *It's your own damn fault. You said you were going to call first.* Yes, call to give Will time to send his lover home before Jack the idiot showed up.

He *had* been planning on calling, but somehow couldn't think of what to say. He'd decided it would be better, as he had last time, just to swing by. Keep it casual—*I was in the neighborhood...*

He'd spent the day in his workshop, finishing the rocking

chair and working on plans for a desk. He hadn't been able to lose himself as he usually did in his work, instead obsessing about Will and whatever was happening between them. The minutes had dragged by endlessly until he'd finally given himself permission to shower and make the drive from New Rochelle to Scarsdale.

Seeing Will and the handsome black man locked in an embrace, heads bowed together in the kiss at his front door, had ripped through him like a knife plunged into his gut. Not that he should have been surprised. Will probably had men lined up around the block waiting to see him. He'd as much as told Jack he played around. Why should Jack be surprised?

Because of what they'd shared. Surely it had been different from the casual play to which Will had referred. Or so Jack had foolishly thought.

He'd been so shocked at the sight of the two lovers, kissing in broad daylight at Will's doorstep, that he'd driven right on by. He had no idea if Will had seen him or not. He only knew he couldn't have faced him right then. He couldn't have borne whatever lies Will came up with, or didn't come up with, to excuse or explain what he'd just witnessed.

Some words Will had said came into his head now, and he understood them on a deeply personal, painful level. *If you don't fall in love, you can't fall out of it.* If only he could fall out of it. That would be much easier than this sickening feeling of humiliation. Jack was just another notch on Will's belt—that much was clear now. He'd been gone a day and already Will was playing the field, lining up the men to keep him safe from any real emotional connection. Whatever Jack had wished, the fact was Will was too immature to connect to anyone, least of all him. He'd been deluding himself, desire clouding a normally rational, realistic outlook.

Go home, back to South Side where you belong, Jack Crawford. Learn from this. At least you've recovered the capacity to feel, even if it hurts.

He turned at the corner and began to drive back the way he had come.

It could definitely be Jack's truck, Will thought. No one who lived on this street drove such a vehicle, instead favoring their SUVs and sports cars.

Will was no exception. He raced into the house and grabbed his keys and wallet, sprinting out the door to his Lexus IS 250. If that had been Jack, he must have seen Paul, he must have seen the kiss. Damn that Paul. Damn Jack for not calling first. Damn the rotten timing of the whole thing.

He pulled out of his driveway and drove as quickly as he dared down the residential street in the direction the truck had gone. At the stop sign he turned left, as the truck had done. He saw it up ahead, disappearing around a corner as he made a turn. He pressed the gas, eager to catch up. He would just explain what had happened, if that's what Jack had witnessed to cause him to drive away.

As he closed in on the truck, he slowed, suddenly wondering what he thought he was doing. Instead of following Jack, he should just call him. He reached for his cell phone and realized he'd left it at home in his study.

They approached the Bronx River Parkway and Jack eased onto the entrance ramp. Not knowing what else to do, Will followed, though still at a distance. They exited after a mile or two, wending their way along various suburban roads until they came to a comfortable middleclass neighborhood, many of the lawns filled with children's toys and bicycles, the houses well-tended if a bit shabby.

The truck turned into the driveway beside the last house on the block, a white stone two-story house with red brick trim. The lawn was tidy and recently mowed, a large oak tree shading the front of the house, its trunk surrounded by bright yellow daffodils.

Will pulled up in front of the house and sat, wondering what to do next. He watched Jack climb out of the truck. Jack turned, catching sight of Will's car. He stood very still for a moment and then turned abruptly away, heading toward his front door.

Will jumped from the car. "Jack, wait."

Jack kept walking, but when he got to his front door, he turned again. He waited as Will raced up to him, out of breath, feeling very foolish.

"Were you following me?" Jack said, his voice cold.

"I was, yes. I forgot my damn phone. Why did you drive away? Why did you come to my house and then just drive away?"

Jack peered at him with those deep-set eyes until Will looked away, his face burning. Determined, he looked back. "Listen, it's not what you think. Whatever you think you saw—"

"You don't owe me any explanation."

"Yes, I do. Of course I do. Come on, Jack. Don't do this. Don't shut me out. Please."

Jack paused and Will could see him struggling. Hoping to push past his defenses, perhaps lowered for a moment, Will touched his arm. "Please, Jack. That was just Paul. He means nothing to me. He had just stopped by. When he left, he kissed me. That's all you saw." Jack didn't respond. Will hurried on. "I was waiting for *you*. Not him. Please. You have to believe me. Don't shut us down. Don't use Paul as an excuse to end us before we've begun."

Jack nodded slowly. "Come inside if you want." His voice was still guarded, his bearing stiff, but at least he hadn't sent Will away. Will followed him into the house. A front hall opened onto a warm, comfortable room filled with wooden furniture with clean, curving lines, upholstered in bright yellow fabric. Jack gestured toward a sofa and two matching chairs. The chairs were large and comfortable, the frames made from polished cherry wood.

"Did you make these pieces?"

"I did." Jack gave a modest smile. "I made just about everything in this house, over the years."

Forgetting for a moment their misunderstanding, Will breathed, "You are *kidding* me. This stuff is museum quality. It's absolutely gorgeous."

"No, no." Jack shook his head. "It's just functional. I use high quality wood and I get it upholstered professionally. It's just a hobby, though. I could never make a living at it. I spend way too much on the raw materials."

"Well, I beg to differ. I'm not saying you should make a living at it. I mean, it must be very labor intensive. But I know people who would think nothing of dropping ten thousand dollars for a chair they admire. If you got into the right market, you could definitely sell this stuff for a substantial profit."

"It's not always about how much you can make off something, Will. Not everything is about gain and the bottom line."

Will was stung by this remark, wondering if there was underlying meaning in the rebuke. He said nothing.

His voice more gentle, Jack said, "Can I offer you a drink? A beer or some soda or something?"

"A beer would be good."

Jack's kitchen was considerably smaller than his own, with white cabinets, a black and white checkered floor and bright yellow walls hung with framed cross-stitch truisms including, "Housework never killed anyone, but I'm not taking any chances," and "God blesses this house, but He doesn't clean it".

Jack, following his gaze, laughed apologetically. "Those are Emma's. She hated housework. She loved to cross-stitch though. It relaxed her, same as building furniture relaxes me, I guess. Her stuff is all over the house. She must have made over a hundred pillows."

"You miss her, huh."

"Yeah, I do."

Jack took a can of seltzer for himself and a can of beer for Will from the refrigerator. He handed the can to Will. "Not fancy imported stuff like you have, sorry."

"Oh stop. This is perfect."

They went back into the living room and settled on the comfortable, elegant chairs. Will stroked the shiny, curving wood of the chair's arm as he tried to formulate what he should say. He decided on the plain, bald truth.

"Jack, that guy you saw, his name is Paul. We work out together. He's also my, uh, play partner from time to time. You know, we have sex. Or we did. Before you and me, that is. I told you, I've never lied to you about it. My sex life has been just that, until you came along. A *sex* life. Not a love life. Paul was a part of that life. He stopped by unannounced. I told him I was waiting for a phone call. As he was leaving, he grabbed me and kissed me."

"You haven't told him about me," Jack interjected. It wasn't a question.

Will felt his face warm as excuses bubbled in his mind. Again he decided on the truth. "No. I haven't. I haven't told anyone." As Jack started to bristle, Will hurried on. "Not because I'm embarrassed or anything like that. No, the opposite is true. What we have, whatever it is that's developing between us, I don't want to share it. Not yet. It's so new, so fragile. What happened between us today is proof of that, I suppose. And what happened yesterday morning. I mean, the way you practically ran out of my house, after such an amazing night."

It was Jack's turn to color. Will waited a beat for him to offer his excuse, but he kept quiet, so Will continued. "I think you left because you're scared, same as me. We both want what's happening, but it matters almost too much. Neither of us knows quite what to do with it. You because you're still struggling with your sexual identity. Me because I've never fallen for someone so hard."

Jack looked up at him, his expression naked and vulnerable for the first time since he'd practically run away the morning before. "Are you saying...you're falling for *me*?"

"Yes," Will whispered. "Yes, I think I am."

Chapter Twelve

"So this is where the master creates," Will said, turning slowly. The room was large and airy, with big windows on two sides through which the sunlight streamed. In one corner of the room piles of wood were neatly stacked by size and type. Sawhorses, various electric saws, lathes and other equipment Will didn't have a name for filled the room. There were shelves filled with bottles of glue and lacquer, cans of paint, trays of nails and screws, sanders and various tools of the trade, all neatly arranged. One corner of the room had been set up as a kind of sitting area, with a low, comfortable couch and an overloaded desk that held a computer and stacks of papers and magazines. Will recognized the onion paper Jack used for blueprints, a blue pen and a pencil resting atop it.

The floor was hardwood, curlicues of sawdust lying here and there. The place smelled of varnish and wood shavings. It was a comfortable, even inviting smell. Will realized it was part of the scent on Jack's shirt when he'd held it to his face—a part of his essence.

"This is my workshop," Jack said, the pride evident in his voice. "I added this room on to the house about ten years ago. Before that I worked in the basement. This is much better. I can actually see what I'm doing. It even has its own door out to the driveway so I can bring in wood and equipment without having to traipse through the house." He pointed toward the door beside one of the windows. A framed cross-stitch with the words, "Jack's Workshop" hung over it.

Jack smiled as he watched Will take in his surroundings. Jack's whole demeanor was more relaxed now that he was on his own turf. Will walked toward the desk and touched the blueprint spread over the papers. "What're you working on now?"

"I just finished a rocking chair that I'm going to give to my sister for her birthday. It's out back so the varnish can dry. I'm going to start on a desk next, actually. To replace this one. I've never made a desk before, so it'll be something of a challenge."

Jack had followed him to the sitting area. Will could feel his presence, hear his voice rumbling close behind him. He turned around and Jack stepped back a little. Will felt vulnerable and needy—feelings alien to him until he'd met this unusual, deeply sensual man.

Silently he willed Jack not to reject his overture. He almost sighed with relief as Jack stepped into his embrace. They held each other a moment, then, of one accord, they leaned in for a kiss.

Will had meant to take his time, to ease his way back into Jack's good graces, but he couldn't seem to help himself. Since Saturday morning when they'd parted, his body had ached for Jack. He'd considered calling Paul or another of his casual play partners for a little meaningless sex, just to take the edge off his need.

Though it was completely out of character, at least for the man he used to be before Jack had entered his world, he'd decided not to. He would wait for Jack. He hadn't even masturbated, clinging to a quaint and rather ridiculous idea of saving himself for his new lover.

Now his lust spilled over. He maneuvered Jack toward the couch, pulling him down as they continued to kiss. Jack, like himself, was wearing a T-shirt and jeans. Will pressed his hands against Jack's strong chest and slipped them beneath the shirt, pushing upward. Jesus, he wanted this man, more than he'd ever wanted another person.

"I have to have you," he whispered urgently. It wasn't enough to fondle and grope—he wanted Jack in the most intimate of ways. He wanted to fuck him and be fucked by him. He didn't just want it—he was desperate for it.

He fumbled at Jack's shirt, lifting it so he could lean down and bite his nipples. Jack looked down at him with an intense expression. His eyes were dark—they looked nearly black, the pupils dilated and fixated on Will's face, his lips parted and wet.

Will fell on him, ravenous, licking and kissing his nipples as his hands slid down Jack's chest, seeking the buckle at his belt. At the same time, Jack grabbed Will's T-shirt and pulled, ripping the flimsy cotton easily with his strong hands. Thrilled by the unexpected and dominant act, Will dropped to his knees on the floor before Jack, his hands still on Jack's belt buckle, which he managed to open. Feverishly he pulled at Jack's fly, licking his lips as he stared at the bulging package in Jack's shorts.

Desperately Will pulled at the boxers, dragging them down so Jack's erect cock and balls appeared, engorged with blood and hard as steel. Will leaned down, one hand gripping the base of Jack's shaft as he lowered his mouth hungrily to lick and suckle his cock.

Jack leaned back against the sofa, murmuring, "Yes. Jesus God, yes, yes, yes..." His fingers twisted in Will's hair, his thighs gripping him on either side as Will worshipped him with his tongue.

It didn't take long. Within a few minutes Jack was panting, his groin thrusting upward as he plunged himself deep into Will's mouth and throat. "Oh, God. I'm going to come. Will, oh, Will." Jack's body trembled, punctuated by spasms and gasps of pleasure as he released his slippery seed, arching in ecstasy. Will held on, milking him until he sagged back against the sofa, his head thrown back, his fingers still entwined in Will's hair, though his grip was now limp.

Gently disengaging himself, Will pulled up beside Jack on the sofa, his cock throbbing. He stared down at his ripped T-shirt and then looked at Jack. Jack had lifted his head and was staring back at Will, lust painted over his face, suffusing his features, making his eyes shine.

"Stand up," Jack said softly, though with a commanding tone Will hadn't yet heard. Intrigued and turned on, Will obeyed. He stood in front of Jack, who reached out and pulled at his fly, popping the snap and dragging the zipper down.

"Take them off," Jack said, his voice low and sure. Was it because he was on his home turf? Or just finally accepting and embracing who and what he really was? Whatever it was, Will's cock hardened even more, if that were possible. He obeyed, dragging his jeans down his thighs along with his underwear. With a shrug he let his tattered T-shirt fall to the ground.

Jack knelt before him, licking his lips, the gesture slow and sensual. He pulled Will forward, his strong, large hands on Will's hips as he parted his lips and closed his mouth over the head of Will's cock.

Will sighed his approval, gripping Jack's shoulders for balance. After several lovely moments of licking and sucking the sensitive crown, Jack leaned forward, trying to take more. He reared back, gagging. Will could feel his frustration. "Use your hand," he offered. "You don't have to take the whole thing in your mouth."

"Sit down," Jack answered. "It might be easier for me." He pulled Will forward, guiding him toward the sofa. Still on his knees, he turned toward Will.

Will leaned back, spreading his thighs as Jack maneuvered between them. Jack took the shaft into his hand, closing his lips over the head. As he lowered his mouth, he lifted his hand to meet it. Will scooted forward to the edge of the sofa to give Jack better access. To his surprise, Jack slipped a finger between his ass cheeks, probing at the cleft.

Will gripped the cushions on the sofa and pushed down against the digit, wishing it were Jack's cock. Jack pulled his hand away, but only to lick his finger and return it to Will's nether hole. He pressed his thick finger inside to the first knuckle and Will couldn't contain his moan of approval.

Jack began to suck faster, his hand flying up to meet his mouth, the delicious friction rapidly bringing Will to the edge. Dimly he was aware of a ringing sound, but he didn't pay much attention, too focused on the roiling pleasure that nearly consumed him. When Jack slipped a second finger into his ass, Will shuddered and began to buck out of control.

Jack pulled his hot mouth away, but his hand continued to fly over Will's cock as Will moaned with pleasure. "Jack!" he cried as he came. "Jack!"

After a moment Will managed to open his eyes, drinking in the sexy sight of his lover, his dark hair falling over into his eyes, his face and throat ribboned with pearly ejaculate.

"Oh. My. God."

Will startled at the sound of a stranger's voice. He glanced rapidly toward the doorway of the workshop, instinctively crossing his legs over his bare sex. His jeans were out of reach, caught beneath Jack's knees. The young man who stood in the door was perhaps twenty-two or -three. Though his hair was lighter and his eyes a different color, there was no doubting this was Jack's son.

Before Will could even wipe his sperm from Jack's face, Jack's head swiveled toward the sound of his son's voice. The young man's face was a frozen mask of horror.

"Eric." Jack's voice was faint. "I didn't hear you come in."

"Obviously," Eric hissed, his face mottled with splotches of dark red as he looked from his father to Will and back again.

"Wait for me in the kitchen."

His eyes narrowed with disgust, Eric raked his gaze over Will and his father before turning on his heel. He slammed the door so hard it rattled in its frame. Will could hear the little ass clomping dramatically away.

Jack pulled himself up onto the sofa beside Will. He was pale, a film of perspiration on his forehead and upper lip. He looked like he was going to pass out.

Dragging his hand over his forehead, Jack said unnecessarily, "That was my son. My younger son, Eric."

"I gathered," Will said, trying but failing to smile. Jack sat still as a stone for at least half a minute. Will meanwhile retrieved his underwear and jeans, the endorphins from his recent orgasm nullified by the shock of the situation.

"You okay?" Will reached out to wipe a gob of semen from Jack's cheek. Abruptly Jack pushed his hand away. He put his own hand to the spot and then looked at his fingers.

"Jesus." He sounded dazed. "I've got to go talk to him."

He stood awkwardly and began to walk, his movements jerky and uncoordinated, as if his nervous system and muscles had gone on strike. He didn't look back at Will. He didn't ask him to wait, or for that matter, to go.

At the door he did finally turn back. “I’m sorry,” he whispered. “I’m so sorry.” Then he was gone.

Will sank back against the sofa. Was he just supposed to leave? Was this it? Had Jack been caught out and so now it was all over?

Will recalled now the ringing sound he had heard, realizing it must have been the doorbell. He thought of his own parents’ house. He too, would have rung the doorbell to be polite, but then let himself in, though he would have called out his arrival. Maybe Eric had called out too, but they hadn’t heard, so intent on each other as they had been.

Jesus, what a mess. What a stupid, ridiculous mess. Will didn’t like messes. He liked things neat and orderly. He most especially didn’t like to be judged, not by some snot-nosed little punk who *disapproved* of his father’s choice in a partner. Disapproval, or more accurately, outright horror and disgust had been painted on his face as clear as day.

What a shock to discover your father was a faggot, Will thought bitterly. Of course Jack hadn’t broken the news to his family. Things were far too new for that. How would Jack respond to being caught? Would he deny what Eric had seen with his own eyes? Would he deny it not only to Eric, but to himself as well?

He wanted to run after them, to beg Jack not to betray what they had by lying or trying to make excuses for what had occurred in the privacy of his own home between two grown men. He wanted to scream it was none of Eric’s business, or anyone else’s for that matter.

Tears pricked Will’s eyes. A sexy, wonderful moment had been ruined, destroyed perhaps beyond repair. *If you don’t fall in love, you can’t fall out of it. More importantly, you can’t get hurt.* Will hurt now, and bad. He leaned over, dropping his head into his hands.

He wanted to follow them into that bright little kitchen. He wanted to defend Jack and himself, to tell that kid he had some nerve just walking in on them. But he knew in his bones Jack wouldn't welcome him coming to the rescue. No, Will was expected to wait, abandoned and alone, while Jack dealt with his demons on his own terms. If that meant shutting Will out and cutting him loose, Will would have to deal with it. What choice did he have? He would have to trust Jack had the courage and honesty to be true not only to his son, but to himself.

They moved automatically toward the kitchen table, the spot where all serious family issues had been hashed out over the years and, ultimately, resolved. Of all the days for Eric just to show up, unannounced. Eric lived in New Jersey, where he worked in the human resource department of a large electronics firm. He usually called before he made the trip up to New Rochelle. The last several times, since he'd become engaged, he always brought his fiancée, Lisa, with him.

Jesus, was she here too? Panic assailed Jack afresh. Why did he feel like an errant child in all this, coming to the table to hear his punishment decreed? He was in his own house, after all. He was a grown man. It wasn't like he was cheating on Emma—he was free to do as he liked.

But not like this—not to be caught with a naked *man*, that man's semen dripping off his face. Jack flushed, deeply embarrassed at what his son had witnessed.

Eric was waiting for him at the table, his face baleful with reproach. "I'm just in shock, Dad. What would Mom say? I can't *believe* I saw what I saw."

Jack lowered himself into a chair, suddenly feeling very old.

"Is Lisa here?" he asked, as much to put off this inevitable confrontation as anything.

"No. We're—we're taking a break. From each other. She needs"—his voice twisted into a sneer though Jack was sure it was to hide his pain—"her *space* for a while, she says. Whatever the hell that means."

"I'm sorry," Jack offered, sorry for his son, but glad for the momentary distraction of someone else's problems.

Eric waved his hand dismissively. "Forget it. We'll work through it. That's hardly the issue now. I want to know what the hell is going on *here*, Dad. Have you lost your mind? I can hardly believe the sickening display—"

"That's enough, Eric." Jack's embarrassment was replaced, or at least partially offset, by rising irritation. Who was Eric to judge him? What did he know of Jack's life since his wife had died? What did he know of life, period?

Still, he knew it must have come as a terrible shock, to see your father, of all people, with another man. He looked at his son. Eric had always been the more intense of the two boys, taking life's random foibles personally. Where Jason could laugh off bad fortune, Eric absorbed it into himself. Privately Jack and Emma used to wonder how they'd ended up with such a serious, sometimes morose boy. He'd been surprised but pleased to learn of Eric's engagement two months before. Lisa seemed good for him—cheerful and gentle, easing him out of funks when no one else could.

"Look, son, whatever you walked in on, you did come in uninvited—"

"Oh, so now I need a personal invitation to my own house," Eric retorted heatedly. "When Mom was alive I didn't need an invitation. I grew up here. I guess I always thought this would be my home."

"Stop it, Eric. Of course it's your home."

"Well, I don't expect to come to my own home and see my father sucking off some—some male prostitute." Eric's face twisted again. He looked as if he might cry.

Jack tried to stay calm, reminding himself he had twenty-three years of experience on the boy. "That wasn't a prostitute, Eric. He was my friend. Is my friend."

"Your *friend,*" Eric sputtered, his voice rich with disdain. "He looked my age, for God's sake."

"He's thirty, if it's any of your business." Jack spoke sharply. He forced himself to take a deep breath. He needed to find a way to explain things without upsetting Eric further.

"Oh, so it's not my business that my father's turned into a fucking *faggot*—" Eric's voice raised to a squeal.

"That's *enough*!" Jack shouted, smashing his fist onto the table between them. Forgetting for the moment about his son's feelings in the matter, he went on, "You don't know what it's like, Eric. To be alone after spending your life with someone. I didn't plan on getting involved with another man. It just sort of—happened."

"You just sort of happened to have your mouth on his dick, is that it?"

Rage hurtled up through his gut like a bitter fire. Barely able to contain it, he said in a soft, dangerous voice, "Eric, I'm going to ask you to leave now. We can talk again when you've calmed down. I will not have you sit in my house and insult me." The tips of his ears burned. He knew he must be crimson. He pressed his nails into his palms to keep from screaming.

Eric pushed back from the table, sending the chair behind him crashing to the floor. "Thank *God* Mom didn't live to see this. Wait until Jason finds out. Jesus, my own *dad*." He stumbled from the kitchen. Jack made no effort to follow him.

The front door slammed and tires squealed in protest down the driveway.

For several minutes Jack sat slumped over the table, his head in his hands. Though he knew it was unfair, a part of him wanted to blame Will—if only he hadn't followed Jack home. If only he hadn't seduced him in the first place. No. That wasn't fair. Jack was a grown man. He hadn't been seduced—he'd gone willingly into whatever the hell it was he and Will shared.

Will...

With a start he realized he'd left Will alone the workshop. Jumping from the table, he hurried through the living room but when he got there, Will was gone. Jack spied the pale green T-shirt he'd practically ripped from Will's sexy body in his lust. It lay on the floor in a puddle, the only proof Will had been there at all.

Jack stepped toward it, bending down to grab it. He clutched it in his fist, dragging it over his face. He could smell Will on it—his particular citrusy, spring soap sort of scent with an underlay of pure masculine musk. The scent evoked Will's presence so strongly Jack nearly cried out his name. He bit his lip instead, so hard he almost drew blood. With a heavy heart he walked to the door that led outside and opened it. Will's fancy sports car was nowhere to be seen.

"What have I done?" Jack said aloud.

He reached into his pocket and flipped open his cell phone. He punched in Will's number and waited, his heart beating jerkily. Instead of Will, he got his voice mail. Having no idea what to say, he hung up.

He moved slowly, feeling as if he'd been in a fight. He felt battered and bruised as he hauled himself through the room. He was heading toward the liquor cabinet, which he hadn't touched since he'd confessed to Anna he might be a drunk.

He opened the cabinet door, reaching behind ancient bottles of tonic water and bitter lemon for the unopened bottle of bourbon a customer had given him along with payment for a job. Not even bothering with a glass, he took the bottle with him to his recliner and sank into it. He twisted off the cap and tipped the rim to his lips, glad for the burn as the liquor went down.

When Will got home, he retrieved his forgotten cell phone. He saw the missed call from Jack and sighed with relief. He'd called. He pushed the button to call him back, pressing the phone to his ear as he sank onto the sofa in front of the fireplace.

"You've reached Jack Crawford of Affordable Improvements. I'm sorry I can't take your call at this time..."

Will closed his phone. He didn't want to leave a message. He checked his own voice messages, but there was nothing from Jack. Damn.

A part of him was tempted to get into his car and drive straight back to Jack's house. When Jack had gone to the kitchen with his son, Will had waited several minutes for him to return to the workshop. When he'd heard the raised voices, the word *faggot* drifting to his ears, his brain had done a temporary short circuit, and he'd found himself in his car, his hand shaking as he tried to fit his key into the ignition.

On the twenty-minute drive home, he'd had time to collect his thoughts somewhat. He realized he shouldn't have run away. Jack was definitely going to be in need of a sympathetic ear once his bigoted son quit the scene.

He stopped himself. The two of them had gotten themselves into trouble in the past by not calling first. Better to let Jack know he wanted to come back. Better to gauge if Jack even *wanted* him to come back. For all he knew, Jack might have done a one-eighty, succumbing to his son's invective—claiming temporary insanity for his lapse of heterosexuality.

Before he could think himself out of it, Will flipped open his phone and called Jack again. Again it went to voice mail, Jack's gravelly, sexy voice apologizing for being unavailable. Damn it. Where was he? This time Will left a message.

"Jack? It's Will. I'm worried about you. Please call me." *I love you.* He wanted to add those words. He very nearly did, biting them off at the last second. Maybe Jack wasn't ready to hear them, especially not now. Will wondered if Jack was ready to *feel* them, but he knew it was too late for that.

He sat, waiting, too jittery and distracted even to go get a fresh shirt from his bureau. He sat for ten minutes, for twenty, for an hour. Still Jack didn't call him back. He thought of calling again. Maybe he hadn't gotten the message? Maybe Eric had only just finally gone. Or maybe he was still there?

Will punched in the number one more time, telling himself this was it. He wasn't going to sit like a lovesick idiot, pining for someone who might no longer want anything to do with him.

He glanced at his watch. It was nearly nine o'clock. He hadn't had any dinner but he didn't feel hungry. He felt numb. And angry. Where the fuck was Jack?

His cell phone rang and Will's heart flip-flopped. Without looking at the Caller ID, he answered. "Hello? Jack?"

"No," the person on the other end said slowly. "Who is Jack? Is he the one you had plans with tonight, eh?"

Will recognized Paul's voice. Embarrassed, he admitted, "Yeah."

"Well, maybe you can bring him too. Francois has four tickets. I thought I'd give you another chance. God knows when you'll get another one. Want to come to Torch with us? You can bring your new boy toy, I promise I won't be jealous." Paul laughed, a long, musical trill along a scale.

"No. No thanks," Will said dejectedly.

"If you change your mind, we aren't leaving for another half hour or so. Francois is *dying* to meet you, darling." Again the musical peal of laughter and then Paul rang off.

Will tried once more, pushing the speed dial for Jack's number. After the fourth ring it went to voice mail. The bastard, he thought, anger rising at last to obliterate the sadness. *He could at least call me. Let me know what the hell is going on. He owes me at least that.*

Anger felt better than sorrow, a lot better. Grabbing onto the emotion like a lifeline, Will again flipped open his phone. "Paul? If it's not too late, I'd like to take you up on that invitation. Just me, though. Jack can't make it."

Chapter Thirteen

The room pulsed with a techno beat, colored lights flashing in time to the music. The place was packed—wall-to-wall men, most clad in denim, silk or leather, some with no shirts, showing off their Bowflex bodies to any and all who cared to ogle them.

Will felt at once at home and entirely alien. Had it really only been a few weeks since Jack had entered his life, capturing his emotions and stealing his heart? There was nothing particularly special about this club, except that it was the hot spot this week or this month.

Next month a new place would crop up, or an old place would be recycled and all these beautiful people would stampede off in that direction, eager to be on the cutting edge of the latest trend.

Paul was wending his way toward Will, his hands held high, some kind of fruity martini in each. Francois was just behind him. Francois was swarthy, his hair dark and cut long, his eyes nearly black in an olive-toned face. He was good-looking, in a desultory, dangerous sort of way, his mouth twisted in a perennial sneer some might regard as sexy.

They stood together, watching the crowd as they sipped their drinks. "Francois and I are going to check out the pit in a while. Want to come?" Paul laughed, adding, "No pun intended."

Will managed a smile, though he didn't answer. He wasn't sure he was in the mood for random sex with strangers. On the other hand, maybe it was just what the doctor ordered. He downed his drink and said, "Next round is on me. More of the same?"

"No more for us, thanks," Francois interjected, his accent rich and pleasing. Paul looked at him with adoration as he continued, "Paul and I want to savor the moment, you understand, *cher*. To keep our blood free from too much alcohol, if you comprehend me."

"What he means," Paul said with a sly grin, "is we want to be able to get it up, eh, Francois?" He nudged Francois in the ribs with his elbow. Francois looked momentarily confused but then smiled and nodded.

"*Exactement.*" He cupped the crotch of Paul's tan leather pants.

Paul pressed against his hand, speaking in a loud stage whisper into Will's ear, "Isn't he simply *fantastique*?"

"You two go ahead. Maybe I'll join you later," Will said. "I'm going to get another drink."

He pushed his way to the bar and raised a finger to catch the bartender's attention. While waiting for his second martini, a man beside him spoke. "I know this sounds like a line, but you have the most beautiful green eyes I've ever seen."

Will turned toward the voice, which was low and sensual, the accent British. The man had dark auburn hair and a luxuriant curling red mustache beneath a long, slightly hooked nose. He was probably in his late thirties and wore a tailored jacket of raw pale blue silk over a black silk T-shirt. His eyes were periwinkle blue beneath heavy brows.

"Thanks." Will smiled. "I love your accent." The bartender set his drink before him and Will took a sip. How familiar this felt—the old pick-up routine. They'd chat a while about what they did, who they knew, where they'd been. The talk would become increasingly filled with innuendo and sly hints that carried the promise of sex.

If the conversation managed to last more than twenty minutes without Will succumbing to boredom, and if the guy was good-looking or interesting enough to capture his imagination, he would end up in bed with him before the night was over.

"I've never been here before," the man offered. "I'm not from New York. Just here on business."

"So I guessed."

The man held out his hand. "I'm Andrew. Andrew Cunningham-Winchester, at your service."

"That's quite a mouthful. I'm Will," he added, shaking the man's offered hand. "Will Spencer."

"Spencer, hmm?" Andrew's smile broadened considerably. "Are you related to the British nobility of that name?"

"I seriously doubt it." Will laughed. "My great grandfather's name was Spelzinksi or something like that when he arrived at Ellis Island with one suitcase and a hundred Zlotys sewn into the hem of his jacket. The immigration officer asked him how he'd like to be Spencer from now on and he smiled and nodded, with no idea what the guy was saying. Or so the family lore goes."

"You don't say," Andrew answered, lifting an eyebrow. "A nugget in the melting pot that is America, eh?" Leaning close, Andrew's voice suddenly dropped into a low, suggestive register. "I'm going to go down and check out this pit everyone's talking about." He looked Will slowly up and down, his intention clear. "Care to join me?"

Will thought about it. He was mildly curious to see the

setup. Francois and Paul had gone on about it at some length as they'd driven into the city—detailing the sumptuous feather mattresses covered in swaths of velvet and lots of gorgeous naked men, muscles shining with sweat and body oil, waiting on hands and knees...

He doubted the actual experience was quite so exotic. These sorts of scenes tended more along the lines of horny, lonely men with hairy asses desperately humping one another in corners, their eyes squeezed shut as they rutted and grunted in their lust. He'd never personally gone in for public scenes, though he had nothing against sex with strangers.

Still, he was here, after all, in *the* trendy underground gay club of the month, so why not at least check it out? He shrugged. "Why not?"

He downed his drink and followed Andrew toward the back of the room to a large swinging door. They pushed their way through and descended a rather steep staircase. The music here was softer, the room backlit by wall sconces designed to look like flickering candles. Will spied Paul and Francois in a corner, Francois' pants already around his knees, his cock in Paul's mouth, a third man still fully clothed standing behind Francois attempting to kiss his neck.

The room was crowded, the air ripe with the odor of spilled semen, male sweat and a riot of mingled colognes. Men in various stages of undress were huddled in groups, gyrating and groaning. "Reminds me of a place in Amsterdam I used to frequent," Andrew said quietly. Will startled, having almost forgotten Andrew's presence beside him. He turned to him, watching as Andrew took off his jacket and looked around for somewhere to hang it. Hooks had been provided along one wall of the room, already heavy with jackets, shirts and pants. Will found himself wondering if people sometimes ended up with the wrong clothing when they went to retrieve their things.

Andrew returned and pulled Will into an embrace. He'd taken off his shirt as well. His chest was broad and covered with a mat of reddish frizz. Will could feel his erection pressing hard against his thigh. Shorter than Will by several inches, he lifted his face, bringing it as close as he could to Will's, his lips parted beneath the curling mustache, his intent clear. His breath smelled like stale whiskey, cigarettes and onions. Will pulled away, unable to hide his flinch of disgust, suddenly yearning so intensely for Jack he felt faint with it.

"What's the matter?" Andrew said, knitting his brow. "Is something wrong?"

"I'm sorry. I need some air. This isn't my thing. Catch ya later."

Stepping over three men engaged in some sort of complex maneuvering that looked more like a game of Twister than any sex Will was familiar with, he hurried up the stairs and back into the club proper.

Paul and Francois remained in the pit for God knew how long. Andrew, it seemed, had also found a partner or partners, as he too had yet to reemerge. Will glanced at his watch. It was nearly midnight. What an idiot he'd been to do this. Once upon a time he would have drowned his sorrows in meaningless sex, but he found he couldn't do that anymore. Or rather, he didn't want to.

He thought about Jack, alone in his house, or worse, still being harangued and interrogated by his outraged offspring. He shouldn't have left him. He shouldn't have abandoned him as soon as the emotional going got tough.

Maybe I'm just not cut out for this relationship stuff, he thought with a sigh. The two martinis had done their work. Will was tired and depressed. He wanted to talk to Jack. He wanted to see him. Again he glanced at his watch. He pulled out his cell phone, checking for any missed calls or messages. There were none. Jack hadn't called him back. For whatever reason, Jack needed his space tonight. Well, Will would give it to him. If one embarrassing confrontation with his son was enough for Jack to chuck the whole thing, then maybe Will had been fooling himself about what was happening between them.

Though Jack was the older of the two, maybe when it came to this he was still a teenager, too tentative and uncertain to follow his feelings. For the feelings were definitely there, no matter how circumstances contrived to mess with them. Will closed his eyes, recalling how hot Jack had been as he'd ripped Will's shirt from his body, his lust palpable, his desire fierce. How he had thrilled to Jack's newfound assertiveness.

That was no experimenting on Jack's part. The time for that had passed. Jack had wanted Will as much as he wanted Jack—of that he was certain. And beyond the sex—they were friends. He'd left his friend in a time of need, turning inward to nurse his own wounds, forgetting how scary all this must be for Jack.

He flipped open his phone again, sending a text to Paul saying he was going to take a cab home, and to have fun. Outside as he waited to hail a taxi, he tried once more to call Jack. Again he got voice mail. A part of him wanted to go straight to New Rochelle, but his pride got the better of him. If Jack didn't want to see or hear from him, he was damned if he'd force himself on him.

Things would be clearer in the morning. He hoped.

Jack squinted one eye open. His two sons were peering down at him, Eric with a frown, Jason with a look of concern.

"Dad? You okay? Did you fall asleep here?"

Jack shifted in his recliner and groaned. A stab of pain shot through his left shoulder as he moved. He must have fallen asleep on it.

He sat up, pushing his hair from his forehead. His head throbbed and his mouth was dry as cotton. "Boys. What are you doing here? What time is it? I didn't hear you come in."

"It's ten o'clock," Jason answered. "We actually called first, but it went straight to voice mail."

"No, of course you didn't hear us come in," Eric said huffily, talking over his brother. He picked up the empty bourbon bottle from the floor and waved it toward his father. "What's this? We're lucky you didn't give yourself alcohol poisoning or drink yourself into a coma."

"Shut up, Eric," Jason said, taking the bottle from his little brother. "Dad's a grown man. If he wants to tie one on now and then in the privacy of his own home, it's none of your business."

Jack's bladder was bulging uncomfortably. He stood, pushing his way past his sons with a gruff, "Excuse me. There's fresh juice in the fridge. Put on a pot of coffee, will you? I'll be right down." He walked stiffly toward the stairs, refusing to give Eric the satisfaction of anything less than a ramrod-straight back and purposeful stride.

Once upstairs he peed and then turned on the water in the sink. He dunked his head beneath the faucet, letting the cold water wake him up more thoroughly. Jesus, had he really consumed that entire bottle of booze? Was he sliding back to where he'd been those first few months of mourning after Emma's death?

What was he mourning now? The loss of Eric's innocence? Or of his own?

Obviously Eric had filled Jason in on all the sordid details of what he'd witnessed the evening before. Jason, who lived two hours north in upstate New York, was single and a research scientist for a pharmaceutical company.

Jack could just imagine Eric's outraged, frenzied call the night before. "Jason, Dad is a faggot. A filthy, perverted faggot who hires male prostitutes he brings to the house for sex."

Jack was saddened by the realization his youngest son was a bigot. He and Emma had consciously strived to make sure their children not only tolerated but accepted other people's differences. He'd thought they'd done a pretty decent job, but evidently not.

Though he knew this wasn't necessarily fair. Eric was still in shock. Even if he were theoretically tolerant of others' differences, it was quite another thing to see your own father kneeling before a naked man, that man's spunk splashed on his face.

With a sigh, Jack turned off the water and grabbed a towel. He was only putting off the inevitable. Though he didn't plan to tolerate any more of Eric's attitude, he owed his boys some kind of explanation.

In the kitchen the smell of brewing coffee greeted Jack like an old friend. Gratefully he accepted the mug Jason poured for him. "Would you like some eggs or something?" Jason asked. "Or I could make pancakes." He was behaving solicitously, as if his father had been ill or suffered a loss. Eric, on the other hand, was scowling, his arms folded across his chest, stern as a judge.

"No thanks, Jason. There's bread in the bread box. Maybe just a piece of toast, if you don't mind."

Jason nodded, moving toward the old white enamel bread box Jack and he had found at a garage sale for one dollar maybe fifteen years before.

With a touch of nostalgia, Jack recalled how close he and Jason had once been. Like him, Jason loved to scour estate and garage sales, looking for bargains and rare items mislabeled as junk.

Now he wondered sadly what Jason thought of him. Was he as disillusioned as Eric apparently was? As horrified and disgusted as his younger brother to learn what their father really was? Would they lose the sweet easiness they'd always shared? The thought nearly broke his heart.

He and Eric had never been as close, though he'd tried to treat his sons equally. Now the rift between them might never be repaired.

Jason brought his toast to the table, along with butter and jelly. "Thanks." Jack tried to ignore the sharp blade of pain jabbing at the back of his eyeballs. He took a bite of toast but his stomach rebelled and he set it down. He sipped his coffee, thinking how he'd like a hot shower. First he would deal with the boys. Better to get it over and done with.

"Eric." He turned to his younger son. "I take it you've filled Jason in on your little visit last night."

"Yes." Eric's tone was defiant. "I certainly did."

"Eric walked in on a rather private moment. I didn't hear him come in."

"I know, Pop." Jason's expression was sympathetic. "I've told Eric he owes you an apology."

"Which is *ridiculous,*" Eric shouted. "I owe him nothing. He owes me, *us*, an apology."

I owe Will an apology, Jack suddenly thought. *He's the one who's been left out of all this.* He felt in his pocket for his cell phone. When he pulled it out, he realized the battery had died. *Shit.* He'd spent the night nearly drinking himself to death, telling himself Will should be the one to call him, since Will had been the one to walk out.

Maybe he had called. Who knew when his phone battery had died? He was forever forgetting to charge the damn thing.

"Dad, you aren't even paying attention," Eric said sententiously. "This is a serious matter."

The coffee had fortified Jack somewhat. "Look, Eric. I'm sorry you walked in on that. I know it must come as a shock to you both. To tell you the truth, I'm probably more shocked than either of you. What I mean is, and what I started to tell you last night, Eric, is that I hadn't planned on this whole thing.

"If you'd asked me a month ago if I was gay or had homosexual feelings, I'd have said, 'No way, are you kidding?'" Eric choked on his juice. Jason's expression was enigmatic. Jack plowed on. "I was married, for God's sake, for twenty-six years. I never looked at another woman, much less another man."

Eric winced. Exasperated, Jack said more sharply than he intended, "Oh Jesus, grow *up*, Eric. I'm your father, not your son, and this is the twenty-first century, not the eighteenth. Last time I checked it was perfectly legal to be gay. Last time I checked I'd raised you to be tolerant of others' differences, to accept that yours isn't necessarily the only viewpoint or way of life."

Eric had the grace to look embarrassed. "I know. But it's different when it's your own father."

"Okay. I can accept that, I guess. But it's not going to change things. The man you saw me with is named Will. Will Spencer. I met him while doing some work on his home. He's not just some guy I picked up, despite your rude insinuations to the contrary. He's my friend. Maybe the best friend I've ever had. We talk. We really talk, about things that matter. He makes me feel good. He makes me happy. We have an emotional connection I never experienced with anyone before."

"What about Mom?" Eric burst out.

Jack started to lie, to answer with a knee-jerk assurance no one would ever replace Emma. He caught Jason's eye, however, and stopped. Jason's expression was curious. He didn't look at all angry, or even sad or confused. He looked, well, happy. Or perhaps amused was the better word. He certainly didn't appear flustered and upset, as Eric did. Something tugged at Jack's subconscious, but he felt too foggy from his hangover to take much notice. Taking courage from Jason's seeming acceptance, he shook his head.

"What your mom and I had could never be diminished by any new relationship I might have. But I'm not going to lie to you. Your mom and I married when we were babies, you know that. We didn't have a clue about love or life at the time. We fumbled our way through and somehow managed to raise you two boys.

"Maybe we were so busy just 'getting through' things, we didn't take the time to connect. Not in the way Will and I have. Maybe this sort of connection can only happen when you're older. When you've got time to focus on things without life grabbing you in twenty different directions."

"No, I don't think that's necessarily true." Jason looked thoughtful.

Jack glanced at him, suddenly aware of something he'd really known for years, though he'd never had the courage or understanding until now to face it. With a kind of wonderment, he waited for what he knew Jason was going to say next.

Jason's smile was calm. "I have that kind of connection right now. I was going to tell you both, when the time was right. His name"—Jason paused, letting the use of the masculine pronoun sink in—"is Tom."

Chapter Fourteen

Jack thought they would never leave. Poor Eric—he had to feel sorry for him, getting double-whammed like that. Jack was both surprised and not surprised by his older son's revelation. On some level, he realized he'd known for a long time.

For whatever reason, it was clear Eric was more inclined to accept his brother's orientation more easily than his father's. No doubt walking in on Will and him had colored Eric's view. Jack knew it would take time to mend the rift between them, and for Eric to come to terms with things.

But right now he honestly didn't care. Or more accurately, he cared about something—someone—else more.

His sons had stayed over an hour. They probably would have stayed longer, much longer, if Jack hadn't pleaded a headache—which was true—and the need to lie down and rest for a while.

He had no intention of resting. What he wanted to do was leap into his truck and drive as fast as he could to Will's house. What he did instead was plug in his cell phone to the charger and go to the landline in the kitchen to call Will's number.

Will answered after three rings. "Hello?" He sounded somewhat out of breath. Jack had a sudden horrible sensation Will was with someone else, and had run to the phone from that man's arms.

"Will?"

"Jack. Jack. Are you okay?" Will's voice was fraught with relief. Jack gripped the receiver, guilt assailing him.

"Will, I'm sorry. I, uh, I got kind of drunk last night. I didn't realize my cell phone had died. I pretty much passed out, I guess, until I was woken by my sons staring down into my face this morning. They've only just left."

Will gave a small laugh, which was like water to Jack's parched conscience. "Do you think," Jack pressed on, "I could come over? We really need to talk and—"

"*Yes,*" Will almost shouted. He laughed again, this time self-consciously, adding in a more normal tone, "Yes, please do come over. I can't wait to see you."

"I'm just going to jump in the shower to try and clear my head. Then I'll be right over."

"So what did you do last night? I kept thinking of you, driving away with no shirt. I'm sorry about that, by the way, about ripping your shirt."

Will grinned. They were lying on his bed, on top of the quilts, fully clothed except for their shoes and socks. When he had opened the door to Jack, they'd embraced, holding each other tight, neither wanting to let go.

Will had suggested they go into the kitchen for a cup of coffee. Jack had surprised him, asking instead if they could lie down on the bed. "I have a killer hangover," he said sheepishly. "I guess I was trying to drown my sorrows. I'm really very sorry, Will, that I left you alone in the workshop like that. I wasn't thinking clearly."

"I understand, really I do. I was upset at the time, but in thinking it over, what else could you have done? Your son needed you at that point, more than I did. How's he handling it, by the way? Has he 'forgiven' you?" Will used his fingers to make quotation marks in the air. "Or is he going to disown you?"

Jack told Will what had happened the night before and this morning. Will tried to remain serious but didn't succeed, laughing with glee despite himself. "I'm sorry." He put his hand to his mouth. "But I would have loved to be a fly on that wall. I guess I should feel sorry for your son and all, but you have to admit, it's a pretty ironic twist—him lining up his brother so they could both come at you." He dissolved into laughter again and Jack began to laugh too.

"I guess it is funny, in a way. It didn't feel so funny though." Jack's smile fell away from his face. Will was at once contrite.

"I'm sorry. I should be more sensitive. You've really been put through the ringer over this. I hope things will be okay..." he hesitated, almost afraid to say the words, "between us."

Jack responded by pulling Will toward him. They kissed, their lips meeting in a tender press. Jack was the first to part his lips, his tongue licking sensually over Will's before sliding into his mouth in search of Will's tongue.

As they kissed, Will felt something inside him ease. The something that had coiled as tight as a spring inside him the moment Eric had uttered his exclamation of horror. He wrapped his arms around Jack and clung to him as they kissed.

When they finally fell apart, Jack said, "What did you do last night?"

Will started to say, "Nothing." Instead he said, "At first I waited for you to call me back. I sat on my sofa, feeling sorry for myself, checking my cell phone every few minutes to see if maybe I missed a call."

"Oh, Will. I'm so sorry—"

"No. Don't apologize. You've already explained and I accept it. I want to be honest though. I want us both to be as honest as we can going forward. You should know, I mean, I've said it before, but it bears repeating, I've never been in a committed relationship before. I'm not even sure I know how to do it, but I want to try. I have this feeling the first step is being honest, even about things we might like to slide over and forget."

Jack's face had become guarded while Will made his speech. Will realized Jack was leaping to his own conclusions. "*No.*" He touched Jack's massive, sexy chest. "I didn't do anything. I can see on your face that's what you're thinking. I didn't go to another man, I promise." He smiled as Jack's face lost its closed, vacant look.

"Okay," Jack said softly. "So what did you do after you gave up on me calling back?"

"Paul and his latest boy toy, this guy named Francois, they invited me to go along with them to this private club. It's called Torch. It's in Manhattan. The latest private trendy club for horny gay guys to engage in shallow, meaningless sex with strangers."

He laughed ruefully, all too aware that until very recently he wouldn't have hesitated to leap into the fray. "I decided what the hell—you'd abandoned me."

"Will—"

"I'm sorry. I'm being a drama queen, ignore me." Will grinned and continued. "The place held the usual crowd of beautiful people and wannabes. This British guy with a hyphenated name tried to pick me up. I realized I just wasn't into it and I left."

"You left? Alone?"

In mock exasperation, Will cuffed Jack's head. "Yes, alone. I caught a cab and came back home. I went to bed, chaste as a lamb, dreaming of you."

Jack raised an eyebrow. "I don't think of you and chaste as words that go together."

"I'm pure as the driven snow." Will pressed his hands together beneath his chin, as if in prayer.

Jack reached out to cuff Will in turn. Will blocked his arm and swiped back at him. In a moment they were locked in a tussle, first one then the other gaining the upper hand. They rolled on the bed, trying to catch one another in wrestling holds.

Jack, though the shorter, was in fact the stronger of the two. Within a few minutes he'd pinned Will beneath him, his knees resting firmly on Will's arms as he straddled Will's hips.

They were both breathing hard and laughing. "You give up?" Jack panted. Will probably could have twisted his way out of it, but he found he liked the weight of Jack on him, holding him down. It made his cock hard.

"Yes," he gasped. "You win."

With a low, throaty chuckle, Jack leaned down. This time the kiss wasn't gentle. Keeping Will pinned beneath him, he claimed him, his tongue darting and swirling in Will's mouth and over his lips. When he reached back, finding and cupping Will's stiff cock beneath his jeans, Will moaned and arched up.

Who was this new Jack, so self-assured, taking what he wanted as if he'd been doing it all his life? This was the same man who had ripped Will's shirt in his lust. What would have happened last night if the outraged son hadn't made his inopportune appearance? Will, used to being in control with whoever he was with, was both excited and a little nervous at the change in Jack's personality.

When Jack finally released his mouth he sat back, Will's arms still pinned beneath his knees. Trying to regain a modicum of control, Will said, "Open your pants. Let me suck your cock."

Jack stared down at him, his eyes blazing with an intensity barely contained, like a flame behind glass about to shatter. Large, thick fingers moved with surprising grace, unsnapping and unzipping. Without even taking down his boxers, Jack pulled out his thick, hard cock and thrust it toward Will's face. Will opened his mouth wide, his tongue flat against his lower lip in invitation.

Jack lifted Will's head, the gesture curiously gentle, as he placed his erect shaft into Will's eager mouth. Will closed his eyes and wrapped his lips around the hot, pulsing rod, licking and kissing it as he opened his throat to receive Jack more fully.

Jack groaned, his hand still cradling the back of Will's head. "Yes, yes." He began to move, pressing his cock deep into Will's throat until the head lodged there, blocking Will's ability to breathe. He didn't care. He wanted Jack to stay as he was, claiming him in this primal, erotic way. He knew he would pass out before he struggled for breath.

Jack pulled back though, allowing Will to catch his breath before he slowly pressed deeper again. "I've never experienced anything like this," Jack breathed. "It just feels so fucking good. I can't imagine anything better."

"I can," Will said, when Jack pulled back enough to allow him to speak. "My ass, Jack. I want you to fuck me."

"I don't know."

Sensing Jack's shift in mood, Will tilted his body and Jack rolled away from him, falling to the bed beside him, his cock still poking invitingly from his shorts.

Will stroked Jack's exposed penis, reveling in its girth and firmness with his fingers. "It's okay. You don't have to know. I'll guide you. I want it, Jack. I want that connection between us."

"I don't want to hurt you—"

"It doesn't hurt. Not when it's done right. It feels great. It's fantastic. Trust me on this. I know what I'm talking about."

"I don't know if I could let anyone do that to me," Jack said, his voice hesitant, even anxious.

"That's why you'll start this way. You do *me*. I'll teach you. Then later, if and when you want it, and only then, I can show you how good it feels in kind." He leaned over and kissed Jack. "You trust me, don't you?"

"Yes. I do."

"Good. That's all you need. Trust." Will tugged gently at Jack's jeans, guiding them down the powerful thighs and pulling them from his body. Gripping the waist of the boxers, he slid those off as well. Leaning back up over Jack, he unbuttoned his shirt and pushed it open.

"Jesus, you're hot."

Jack turned his head on the pillow, embarrassed at the praise, though Will noted his erection never flagged.

Sliding to the edge of the bed, Will stood a moment to shuck off his own clothing, discarding it in a heap on the floor before returning to the bed. His cock was bobbing toward Jack and, unable to help himself, he gripped it, stroking himself as he lay beside his lover.

"I want you, Jack. Do you want me? Do you want to take our exploration to the next step?"

"I don't know." Jack bit his lip. Will noted his cock was still hard as granite, despite his protests. Deciding to go off that cue rather than Jack's words, he reached over to his nightstand and pulled a condom from the drawer. Jack made no comment as Will opened the wrapper and rolled the sheath over Jack's erection.

He took the tube of lubricant and squeezed a dollop onto his fingers, which he daubed on the tiny hole between his ass cheeks. Jack's eyes were wide beneath the thick brows. Will lifted himself to his hands and knees beside Jack.

"Get behind me," he encouraged. "Just lean up against me. Get used to the feeling of our bodies touching." Will's cock was throbbing as he waited, silently willing Jack to obey. If he protested again, if he said he wasn't ready, Will wouldn't press. There was time. As eager as he was to feel Jack's cock penetrate his tight heat, he would wait. He would be patient.

Will recalled suddenly a man he'd brought home from a bar once years before. He himself had only been about twenty-four, the other guy barely twenty-one. The guy had turned out to be bi-curious—a complete novice with no real experience with another guy beyond making out in the back of a car a few times.

The man had said all the right things, pretending he'd done way more than he had. It wasn't until they were naked in bed together, Will with a condom on his cock ready to fuck the guy, when he'd admitted he'd never been with a man "in that way" as he'd euphemistically said. He confessed he was scared and not really into anal sex.

Though Will was ashamed to admit it now, after a few half-hearted attempts to make the guy feel more relaxed, he'd pulled on his jeans and told the guy to do the same, irritation over having been tricked outweighing any empathy or understanding.

But that was ancient history, or so it seemed. Will wasn't

the same person and Jack was hardly some guy he'd picked up in a bar. He watched Jack a moment, noting the still hard cock warring with the uncertainty in his eyes. "We don't have to," Will said softly. "Maybe it's too soon..."

Jack slowly shook his head. "No. I want it. I'm just scared I'll hurt you." He knelt up behind Will and Will closed his eyes, eager to feel Jack's hard cock press against him. Instead, to his surprise, he felt Jack's fingertip circling the rim of his asshole, gliding easily against the lubricant.

"It's so tiny, so tight," Jack whispered. The finger pressed gently, slipping past the entrance. Will gasped with pleasure, lifting his hand to his cock to ease the ache there. He tightened his sphincter muscle around Jack's thick finger, trying to suck it in farther. Jack complied, easing his finger farther into the hot grip of Will's ass.

"Am I hurting you?"

"No, no, not at all. It feels wonderful." Will waggled his ass, pressing back against the invading digit. He felt a second finger joining the first, stretching him, and he moaned. "Yes. Don't stop. Yes..." Will massaged his cock, his nerves zinging, ricocheting from his ass to his nipples to his cock and balls with each twirl of Jack's fingers.

He twisted back toward Jack. "Kiss me," he demanded.

Jack complied, leaning up over his back until their lips met. He pressed deeper, his fingers now buried in Will's ass as he bit Will's lips and pushed his tongue into his mouth. Jack was panting, clearly aroused by what he was doing.

"Fuck me," Will urged breathlessly. He was dying for Jack's cock, desperate for it. He was never one to beg, not Will Spencer. He rarely lost his cool, even when the sex was hot. But this was different. He honestly felt if Jack didn't fuck him, and soon, he would die. Never in his life had he wanted something, wanted someone, so much.

"Please," he begged. "I need you."

Jack's fingers were withdrawn. He knelt back on his haunches, his cock in his hand. Their eyes locked as Jack leaned forward, guiding his shaft toward Will's nether hole. When the head touched the entrance, Will shivered. He turned to face forward, resting his forehead on the cool sheets, his ass lifted high and lewdly spread for his lover's invasion.

Jack seemed to hesitate, teasing Will with the head of his cock, which he touched to Will's entrance before pulling back. "Please," Will entreated. "I want you so bad. Please fuck me, Jack. Please."

Jack leaned into him again, the bulbous head of his cock pressing into Will's ass. There was the initial twist of pain, lasting only a second or two, and then...ah...yes... "Jack," Will breathed, pressing back against the invading shaft. He gripped his cock again in one hand, keeping his balance with his forehead and one elbow against the mattress.

Jack was silent for several seconds, holding his position, only the head of his cock nestled in Will's ass. Will tried to remain still, to give him a chance to get used to what he was doing. He failed, fidgeting and wriggling in his effort to impale himself farther on Jack's iron shaft. He nearly whimpered with frustration.

Jack seemed to come alive suddenly, easing deeper into the passage. "God, it's so *tight*. It feels incredible." He moved forward, gripping Will's hips with his hands as he guided himself farther inside. He groaned and Will answered with a moan of his own.

Leaning hard into him, he slid deep inside Will, his balls slapping Will's ass as he thrust forward. He was breathing fast, his thick cock completely filling Will, leaving him breathless and gasping with each swivel.

He wanted to ask Jack if he was sure this was his first time. His movements were so deft, so seemingly calculated to draw every ounce of pleasure from Will's body. But he couldn't form the words. The pleasure was so acute Will had literally lost the capacity for speech. He could only make a series of grunting sounds in time to Jack's thrusts.

He spit on his hand and returned it to his cock, stroking and pulling as Jack moaned and thrust behind him. Will clenched his ass cheeks, milking Jack's cock with his anal muscles. Jack gasped. "Will, what are you doing to me? Oh God, it's so good. It's so fucking good." Jack began to tremble, his cock pummeling Will's ass in a frenzy. His fingers were digging into Will's hips as he thrust hard against him, nearly sending him sprawling.

"Will. Will...I can't... I'm going to...oh..." All at once his body grew rigid, except for the tremor in his loins. He gripped Will hard with his strong fingers, so hard it hurt, momentarily distracting Will from his pleasure. Jack's grip loosened as he jerked and shuddered against him. Will could feel him ejaculating deep inside him. The realization thrilled him, giving him just the push he needed to climax. With a cry, he let himself go, coming into his hand as he called Jack's name.

He let himself fall slowly forward, taking his lover with him. Jack remained buried inside him, his arms wrapping beneath Will's body to capture him in a tight embrace. Will could feel Jack's heart pattering against his back, or was it his own?

They lay like that for several minutes, until their hearts slowed their frantic beat. Will reached again for the nightstand, pulling a small plastic bag and a washcloth from the drawer.

When Jack rolled off him, Will turned toward him, removing the spent condom and dropping it into the trash can beside the bed. Jack flashed him a grateful look.

He wiped the ejaculate from his hand and tried to wipe a blob that had landed on his pillowcase, but gave up with a grin, tossing the cloth aside. Jack lay on his back, his hands crossed over his chest, his eyes closed. Will leaned up on one elbow beside him.

"So, how was it?"

"Incredible." Jack's voice was hoarse, his breathing still somewhat labored. He looked toward Will, his eyes shining.

Will smiled broadly. "I knew you'd like it. I can't believe that was your first time, though. Some of your moves drove me wild."

Jack let out a deep breath. He looked away for a moment, and then back at Will. "Well, it's not all that different from being with a woman. I mean..." Jack blushed slightly, "you know."

"Sometimes I can't believe you're actually in your forties," Will teased. "You're so ridiculously shy about certain things. You mean, it's not so different from vaginal intercourse."

"Well, yes, if you want to get clinical about it, yes." Jack wrinkled his nose.

"I've wondered about that. I've never been with a woman."

"Never, huh? No exploration in the back of the car on a date? Nothing like that?"

"Nope. I've always known my attraction was toward men. Unless you count children's games, I've never even kissed a female."

"I guess that makes sense. Most straight guys have never kissed a guy." Jack grinned.

Will nodded. "I've wondered though, I mean in a casual way, how anal sex is different from vaginal. I mean, it's got to feel different."

"Sure. With a woman it's softer. It's more like a velvet glove sheathing you. A wet, hot velvet glove."

"That sounds nice really."

"It is nice. But with a man, well, from my one time of experience"—Jack laughed, looking embarrassed but happy—"it's more like a vise. It's like this tight ring of pleasure you push into. You have to move more, I guess, to get enough friction." He turned toward Will. "That thing you did with your muscles. That was something else again. That definitely pushed me over the edge."

"I've got lots more tricks up my sleeve." Will waggled his eyebrows à la Groucho Marx. "You just stick with me, I'll blow your world wide open."

Jack smiled but then sobered. "You already have, Will. Believe me."

"I know." An extraordinary tenderness overcame Will, actually bringing tears to his eyes. Blinking them away, he touched Jack's face with his fingers, drawing a line down his jaw.

I love you, he almost said.

Jack sat on the bed in the room he'd shared with Emma for so many years. A picture of the two of them on their wedding day, looking happy, nervous and incredibly young, stared at him from the bureau. Baby pictures of Eric and Jason rested beside them, waving and grinning toothlessly from their frames.

Jack hadn't been back to his place for two days. Will and he had spent a marathon in bed, making love until they couldn't keep their eyes open, or hunger drove them in search of sustenance. Eric and Jason had each called him, Eric wanting to talk some more, "in person", Jason checking in, he said, to make sure he was doing okay.

Knowing he couldn't put it off forever, Jack had agreed to meet Eric that evening at his place. Plus he needed to mow his lawn, check his mail and get fresh clothing. He'd told Will he'd come back that night after what Will had jokingly referred to as the *inquisition* by his son.

Now that he was home, however, he was thinking maybe he should take a day off, as it were. Give them both a chance to catch their breath.

When he was near Will, he couldn't seem to get enough of him. Though he was by far the older of the two, he had turned out to be the more sexually insatiable. Will teased him that he couldn't keep up with him—that he'd have to find another guy to service him when Will wasn't enough.

But he was enough. Never in his life had Jack felt so happy and, more than that, so complete. He hadn't realized he'd spent his life incomplete, like a jigsaw puzzle missing some elemental pieces. Will had placed the pieces in exactly the right spots. Jack could almost feel the wholeness that seemed to exist within him now, a wholeness that had never been there before.

He glanced at Emma's youthful, glowing face, feeling guilty as he admitted in stark terms she had never been enough. Yes, he had loved her, and she had loved him too, but the passion, and even beyond that, the *ease* he felt with Will, were completely new to him.

Though he mourned her death—of course he did—he wondered if he would have spent the rest of his life incomplete, and unaware of this incompletion. Had she felt the same way? Or was such a concept beyond her ken? Was the question even fair? Probably not. Nor was there much point to such speculation.

He had been as good a husband as he knew how to be when she was alive. Now, it seemed, he was about to start a new life, a whole new way of thinking and of being he'd only just begun to grasp.

There was no question it was harder to be involved with another man. Society, at least this society, still frowned and judged, for all its pretended acceptance in the media. Gay men were still the butt of jokes about interior decorators and limp-wristed handshakes. They were still the target of degradation, discrimination and violence, based solely on their sexual orientation.

Even in his own family, the bigotry and misunderstanding existed—Eric a perfect case in point. Even his own reaction, when he'd seen Paul and Will kissing at Will's door, had been one of disapproval beneath the jealousy. Men shouldn't indulge in public displays of affection, certainly not with each other.

And yet, why not? Why was it okay for a man and woman to kiss at their own front door, but not two men? Why could two women walk hand in hand down the street, but not two men?

He was beginning to recognize the courage it took just to be gay in a straight, reactionary society. He couldn't help but wonder if he had the courage it took to face his own feelings honestly.

Would he tell his sisters? Anna, he felt, would understand. But would her husband? Would his other sisters, or his mother, for that matter, who was still alive? Would he bring Will home to family dinners and Christmas Eve? When Eric married, would he bring Will to the wedding as his significant other?

Jack shook his head. He was jumping the gun and he knew it. They had yet to say they loved each other and here he was bringing Will home for family holidays in his head.

Did he love Will?

Yes.

If love meant having your heart clutch with joy each time you saw someone, then yes. If it meant thrilling to their touch, be it casual or sensual, no matter what, then yes. If it meant wanting to protect them and care for them and make them happy, putting those things even before your own happiness, then yes. He loved Will.

While this was exciting, a feeling he never thought he'd experience, indeed, barely knew existed, it was also terrifying. Not just because they were both men, but because Will was so much younger.

He believed Will was sincere in his affection, but how long could it last? They were fourteen years apart. It wasn't an impossible span, but it was significant. They were of different generations. They'd grown up with different music, different life experiences. Jack had been married when Will was only four years old.

Was it possible for two such people to make a life together?

Stop it. Jack punched the mattress, annoyed with himself. Who the hell was talking about making a life together? They'd known each other a month, for God's sake. They'd only been intimate for less than a week.

Live in the moment.

That's what the affirmation book someone had given him when Emma had died had said. It was good advice, he knew. The past was done, the future was unknowable. Just live now, savor the joy that is now.

The doorbell rang and Jack forgot about the joy. Eric was waiting, no doubt ready with a new sermon about his father's "bad behavior". Jack sighed and moved toward the stairs, calling, "Come on in. The door's open."

Chapter Fifteen

"Hey, Dad."

"Eric. Come in." Jack peered at his son. He looked awful—wretched and woebegone. Surely he couldn't be this miserable over Jack. Something else must be wrong. "Son, what's the matter?"

"It's Lisa," Eric said softly. "I called her. You know, about all this. We still talk every night even though she's 'taking a break' as she says." He smiled a bitter smile. "Anyway, I thought she'd understand what I'm going through, but instead she bit my head off." He looked indignantly at his father, as if he were somehow to blame.

They had walked into the kitchen as they talked, the center of family life when the boys still lived at home. Jack raised his eyebrows in question, not choosing to speculate just what Eric meant. He stirred the spaghetti sauce he had simmering on the stove and waited for Eric to continue.

"She said I needed to be more understanding. She said I was a—a bigot. She said I had a lot of nerve treating my own father like that, when I was the one who had invaded your privacy."

"Did she?" Was Eric expecting him to disagree with Lisa?

"Yeah." Eric fell into a chair at the kitchen table. "Jason told me the same thing, but that doesn't count because he's a—

I mean he's also…"

Jack glanced over at his son, almost feeling sorry for him. Why did he have to make things so difficult for everyone?

Eric hit the table with his fist, making the salt and pepper shaker resting on a woven mat at its center bounce. "Damn it, Dad. People don't just suddenly *become* gay. Jason told me he's always known he was—he just never found the right person before. He said he wasn't sure how you and Mom would react so he just kind of kept it to himself. But he *knew.* So what about you, Dad? How long have you been carrying this sick little secret around—two years, five years, *twenty* years?"

Jack suddenly understood, and as a result he was able to let go of the rising anger Eric's words had aroused in him. He slid into a chair opposite Eric. "You must really miss Mom. The two of you were especially close."

Eric's clenched fist loosened and he dropped his head to his chest. "Yeah." His voice cracked. "I do."

Jack reached across the table, gently squeezing Eric's arm, any lingering anger completely given over to compassion. "I didn't plan this, Eric. Of course I would have rather told you and Jason in my own time, on my own terms. I'm still just coming to grips with my feelings myself. It's all very new to me.

"One thing I want you to understand in no uncertain terms. What I feel for Will in no way diminishes what your mother and I shared, or the love I had for her and always will. Nor, though I think you know this, does it affect my love for you and Jason.

"You ask me how long I've known. It wasn't something I kept hidden from the world. Or maybe, to put it more accurately, it was something I kept hidden from myself. Maybe on some level I did know, but I was too shut down, I guess, to handle it.

"Before I married your mom, I had a best friend. His name

was Luke. Something happened between us. Something—sexual. It was fumbling and unplanned and frankly it scared me to death. I rejected him—and the feelings the interaction raised in me. We had a falling out. I put it behind me. I got married so young, I never had a chance to really work those feelings through. I guess they lay dormant in me until I met Will."

"Will," Eric said, a sneer in his voice.

"Eric, you need to stop that. You aren't a child. I wouldn't denigrate or put down someone you were with, no matter who you chose." Forcing himself to remain calm, again he touched his son's arm.

"Eric, I love you. I'll always love you. But the fact is, my life is changing, in ways I never imagined. I'm not going to hide it or shut it off to please you. I'm happy, Eric. My life has meaning. In some ways I'm happier than I've *ever* been. It's like a part of myself has been kept hidden, even from me, until now. I feel it unfolding, full of potential.

"And yes, if you want to know, it's scary as hell sometimes. It's scary to be in a relationship where you really care. Where the other person can make or destroy you with a single smile or by turning away."

"I know," Eric said, his eyes suddenly bright with unshed tears. "I love her, Dad. I love her but I do everything wrong. I'm too possessive, she says. I suffocate her. If she only knew how much I love her, she wouldn't feel that way. Now this, it's just one more nail in my coffin. She says I'm a bigot. I don't mean to be. It was just such a shock. You know, to see your own father like that..."

"I know, Eric. I would have felt strange walking in on you and Lisa."

"It's not the same."

"It's not all that different. Walking in on anyone in the

middle of an intimate moment—"

"Yeah, but—"

"Yeah, nothing. I think you're more freaked out because I'm your father than anything. I know I never thought of my parents as sexual beings until I was married myself. Maybe it's part of growing up to realize they are, whoever their choice of a partner."

Eric seemed to ponder this. "I think I understand. I want to understand. That's why I wanted to come over again. To tell you I'm working on it. I love you, Dad. It may take me some time to get really comfortable with all this, but I'm willing to give it a try."

Jack smiled at Eric, relief flooding him. "Maybe you could let Lisa know we had this talk. Maybe tell her what you just told me. It might go a ways to helping her see you're not a bigot after all."

"You think?" Eric said, his face hopeful.

"I have a feeling the two of you will work things out. If she wasn't interested, she would just have broken things off, instead of 'taking a break' while still talking every night on the phone.

"I've found if you can really listen to someone, to what they're really saying, that's half the battle. Listen to Lisa. Pay attention. If she feels suffocated by the closeness of the relationship, step back, even if it hurts. Because ultimately, when she no longer feels pressured, if the relationship is right, she will come back to you. She'll remember the things she loves about you and she'll give you and the relationship another chance."

Eric looked thoughtful. "Thanks, Dad." He stared down at the table and finally up again at Jack. "Dad?"

"Yeah?"

"I'm sorry. I was kind of a jerk."

Jack grinned. "That's okay. I'm glad we could talk things through. Now, can you stay for spaghetti and meatballs?"

"So how did the talk go?"

Eric had left soon after dinner, eager to call Lisa. Jack in turn called Will. "It went way better than I expected, actually. Eric's starting to see reason, thank goodness. His girlfriend told him he was a bigot. He heard her where he didn't hear me or his brother, I guess. He stayed for dinner. We had spaghetti."

"I'm glad, Jack."

"Yeah." Jack missed Will already, even though they'd only been apart a few hours. It occurred to him the very advice he'd given Eric might apply to his own fledgling relationship. Maybe he was spending too much time with Will. Maybe Will needed a little space, just like Lisa.

The thought was unsettling, even painful. Nevertheless, he decided to test the waters. "I was thinking maybe I'd stay over here tonight."

"How come?" Will asked.

"I've got a job early tomorrow morning, for one thing."

"Okay," Will said slowly. "That's one thing. Is there another thing?" Will's voice was light too, but Jack sensed the sudden strain in it, which no doubt Will sensed in him as well. Was it always going to be this difficult?

"I don't know. You might need a break. Maybe you have some things to catch up on."

There was silence at the other end of the phone. When he

finally spoke, Will's voice was somber, even sad. "Are you having second thoughts, Jack? Is there something I should know about? Did I do something? Is something wrong?"

"*No,*" Jack responded quickly, his heart aching at the pain in Will's voice. "It's just..." He took a breath, and then, determined to be honest, he admitted, "I'm afraid I'm too much. That I'm going to push myself on you and you'll get tired of me and send me away."

There was a silence for a beat or two and then Will burst out laughing. "Jack Crawford, are you insane? I'm crazy about you. I've been missing you like mad since sixty seconds after you left. I was sitting here, feeling jealous of Eric because he was with you and I wasn't, wishing I could have come with you, wishing I was more a part of your life.

"I almost called you like six times over the past few hours. I forced myself not to, probably for the same reasons as you—I didn't want to appear too needy, too grasping. So, no—I can't imagine sending you away as you so quaintly put it. I want you, Jack. I'm in love with you. I've never been happier than in the past few days."

I'm in love with you.

Jack sat holding the receiver to his ear, the words reverberating in his head. *I'm in love with you.*

"Jack? Are you there? Jack?"

Jack recognized the magnitude of the gift Will was offering him. A new chance at happiness, when he'd basically resigned himself to a life alone—had even told himself he was content with his lot. He'd raised his family, he had good, steady work, he had his workshop and his garden...

He'd spent his life doing the right thing and trying to keep those around him happy, without regard to the terrible price he'd paid inside. He wasn't old. He was only forty-four, for heaven's sake. He had half his life left, waiting for him to seize it, to cherish each moment with a man who loved him.

Will was offering him the chance to *live.* Even more important than being loved was the chance to love in return. To let himself be vulnerable, to give of himself in every respect, even knowing his lover had the power to take it away.

No, he wouldn't step back. He wouldn't hide in his comfortable, quiet tomb of a house, pretending, as Will had called him on it, that he was doing it for Will. He would take the risk, all the risks that falling in love entailed. He would trust Will, and even more importantly he would trust himself.

"Jack?"

"Can I come over? Now? I have something to tell you."

Will opened the door to Jack and held out his arms. Jack stepped into them and they kissed.

"Welcome back. What's it been? A week, a month? I thought you'd never get your ass back here."

Jack laughed. "You taste salty."

"I was riding my stationary bike. I was just going to shower. Care to join me?"

"I'd love to." Jack's cock jerked to attention.

They washed each other, taking turns soaping up each other's body, spending extra time on certain areas. Will lathered Jack's cock, gripping it as he leaned down. "I want you, Jack. I want to take you tonight. Is it time? Are you ready yet to receive me?"

A sharp jolt of adrenaline slid through his gut. Ever since they'd first made love, it had remained one-sided. While Jack became increasingly comfortable with penetrating Will, he had yet to be on the receiving end.

It wasn't that he found the idea disgusting or repelling in any way. Quite the contrary—he'd come to crave the intense intimacy the act created between them. He wasn't even entirely clear on the source of his hesitation. He supposed it was part fear of a physical unknown—how could he handle such a huge thing entering such a tiny opening? Surely it had to hurt, no matter what Will said.

When he was honest with himself, he recognized the fear went deeper than any physical consideration. It was such an intimate act—such a complete bearing of oneself. He wasn't sure he had the courage to render himself so completely vulnerable to another person, even if that person was Will.

Jack didn't answer the question directly. Instead he climbed out of the shower, tucked a towel around his waist and took a second, larger towel. When Will stepped out of the shower, Jack wrapped him in the towel, sinking to his knees as he lovingly dried Will's long, sexy legs.

He knew, suddenly, it was a matter of trust. He looked up at his handsome young lover and smiled. "Yes," he announced, trying to ignore the butterflies beating their wings in his belly. "I want it. I want you."

They lay together on the bed, naked in each other's arms. They kissed, their erect cocks colliding. Finally Will disengaged himself from Jack's embrace, sliding down to take his shaft into his mouth. Jack sighed, stunned anew at the nearly unbearable pleasure he experienced each time Will did this. Will licked and kissed along the shaft, his hands stroking and fondling his balls, his fingers exploring the cleft of Jack's ass.

Jack tensed for a second, as he always did when Will touched him there. He knew intellectually this made no sense. He loved touching, probing, exploring Will's intimate passageway—why should he be so shy, so uncomfortable when

Will attempted to do the same?

Trust. He would trust Will to keep him safe, even if it pressed the envelope of his sensual comfort. He lay on his back, permitting Will to push his legs up and back, so his feet were resting flat on the bed, his ass exposed for his lover's attention.

He closed his eyes, taking a sharp breath as Will dipped his head, lowering it past Jack's balls to the tiny puckered hole below. Jack couldn't help the shudder when he felt Will's warm, wet tongue lick along the rim. Despite his anxiety, he had to admit it felt good.

After a while, the tongue was replaced by Will's finger, gently, carefully touching and then entering Jack's nether entrance. His muscles clamped down around it.

"Relax, you're doing great," Will urged. He pressed deeper and Jack found his body adjusting. It didn't hurt. It felt good. He was distracted by Will's other hand curling seductively around his cock.

He felt a second finger stretching him, causing a momentary discomfort that was quickly replaced with a returning buttery pleasure.

"You ready, Jack? I want you so bad."

"Yeah," Jack said, his stomach clenching. He started to get up, to rise to his hands and knees as Will had done the several times they'd had intercourse.

"Why don't you stay like that?" Will suggested. "Lie on your back just like you are. You'll be less likely to tense, I think. And this way I can see your face, gauge how you're doing. Does that sound okay?"

Mutely Jack nodded. Will skillfully rolled a condom onto his erect cock, which he then coated with a liberal squirt of lubricant. He leaned up over Jack, reaching down with still-slick fingers to ready Jack's ass.

Jack closed his eyes. It was easier to relax like this, though he wasn't quite sure of the mechanics of the operation. *Trust Will.* Yes, he would trust Will. He wanted this, as much as, maybe more than Will. He wanted to prove to them both he could do it.

Will lowered his face, kissing Jack's lips before moving up to kiss his eyelids, one at a time. He kissed Jack's forehead and each cheek. He kissed his chin and then slid his tongue sensually down Jack's throat while his hand found and gently gripped Jack's cock.

Jack sighed with pleasure, melting into the mattress as Will stroked and massaged him. He felt Will's fingers again at his entrance, first one, then two. They slipped in. As Will had promised, in this position he found it difficult to tense, even if he had wanted to.

The fingers were soon replaced by the fat head of Will's cock. It nudged against the tight circle of muscle, easing its way inside. Will held himself still, giving Jack's body time to adjust. It felt full but it didn't hurt. Will continued to stroke Jack's cock as he asked, "You okay? You're doing so good, Jack. I'm proud of you."

"I'm okay." Jack's heart was striking a rapid tattoo against his sternum. He was still scared, but very turned on at the same time.

"Good. I want you to bear down against my cock as I enter you. It will keep you from tensing up." He leaned down, kissing Jack's mouth as he pressed slowly forward. There was a sharp, jabbing pain and he gasped. At once Will pulled back, though the head of his cock remained inside Jack. Jack understood what it must be like for young women the first time. He remembered his own frustration their first time, when Emma had stopped him repeatedly, squealing he was hurting her. It had become rather difficult to maintain an erection in the face of her cries. He had wanted to stop but she'd begged him to continue.

He didn't want to put Will in that position. He could handle this—he was a man. "I'm sorry," he said, smiling apologetically. "Don't stop. I want it. Please."

Will nodded and leaned forward. Again Jack felt the jab, but the pain was less intense. He breathed through it and bore down as Will had suggested. The pain eased.

"You did it, Jack. You did it. I'm all the way in. How does it feel?" Will ran his hand up and down Jack's cock as he asked the question, distracting him so completely for a second he forgot to answer.

Finally he said, "Good. It feels good. So full. I feel possessed, somehow, completely possessed in a way I never imagined. I love you, Will."

"I love you, Jack," Will answered. His eyes burning into Jack's, he began to move, drawing his cock nearly out before pressing back, filling Jack, possessing him, owning him. Jack groaned and let all thoughts finally slide out of his over-analytical brain. He gave in to the heavenly sensations of Will's hand and cock.

Will began to move faster, panting above Jack, his eyes now screwed tight. "Unh, unh, unh," he began to chant, the cries punctuating his sensual movements. His hand still gripped Jack's cock, pulling hard with each thrust of his hips.

"Oh, oh, oh..." Will cried, dropping Jack's cock in his frenzy. He smashed against Jack, plunging deep inside him as he fell forward. Jack held out his arms, catching his lover in a tight embrace.

The friction of Will's hard stomach rubbing against his cock was enough to send Jack over the edge as well. He felt his own sticky semen spurting between their bodies as Will shuddered and spasmed in climax against him.

They stayed like that a long while. Jack loved the heaviness of his lover draped over him. He felt if they never moved again, he would be content.

Eventually Jack became aware Will's cock had slipped from his body. Gently he pushed his lover onto his back, removing the spent condom as Will had done for him, tossing it into the small can beside the bed. Will reached for a towel he'd brought beforehand to the bedside. He started to wipe Jack's sticky belly, but his hand fell limp.

"I can't move," he groaned with a small, weak laugh. "You have utterly destroyed me, Jack Crawford."

Jack took the towel and wiped his stomach and Will's too, before using the towel to gingerly wipe his ass. It was tender to the touch but otherwise intact. Along with the endorphins shooting their way like fireworks through his blood, Jack felt something else. Pride unfurled inside him like a flag of victory.

He'd done it. He'd found a way to move past his inhibitions, his fears, his hesitation. He'd found a way to trust, not only Will, but himself.

"You look like the cat that ate the canary," Will said lazily, watching Jack through half-closed eyes. "What are you grinning at?"

"Oh, nothing. Everything." He let out a whoop of joy.

Will look startled. Jack's face heated but he whooped again. Why not? He was happy. Will laughed. "So it was okay, huh? You're not a virgin anymore. What should we do now?"

Jack grinned, his eyes narrowing, his cock, unbelievably, rising with interest at the question. "You know what they say, Will. Practice makes perfect."

About the Author

Claire Thompson lives and writes in upstate New York. She has written over forty novels, many dealing with the romance of erotic submission, along with a newfound passion for m/m erotica.

To learn more about Claire Thompson, please visit www.clairethompson.net. Send an email to Claire at Claire@clairethompson.net and sign up for her newsletter to keep abreast of her latest work, events, happenings and contests.

Liberal vegan meets corporate carnivore.
What could possibly go wrong?

The Happy Onion

© 2008 Ally Blue

Thomas Stone has one sacred rule: Don't Date The Boss. Ever. So when he finds out his new employer is the man he took to bed his first night in town, he's less than happy. He doesn't need any more complications in his life, and the way Phil makes him feel definitely qualifies as a complication. Especially since he can't seem to keep his hands off the man.

Philip Sorrells is thrilled to discover that the new bartender his manager hired for his restaurant, The Happy Onion, is the aggressive little blond he slept with once and can't forget. Thom is Phil's wet dream come true, from his angelic face to his fiery temper. For the first time, Phil hears the siren song of monogamy, and he's tempted to follow it.

When Thom leaves The Happy Onion for a job managing an upscale nightclub, it looks like a chance for him and Phil to be together without the whole boss/employee thing hanging over them. Instead, Thom's new position brings out previously unsuspected differences in their world views. Differences with the power to destroy their fragile bond.

So how will this nature-loving tree-hugger and corporate-ladder climber navigate this political minefield in the name of love? Very carefully.

Warning, this book contains bad language, good music, vegan personal care products and lots of hot, dirty mansex.

Enjoy the following excerpt from The Happy Onion…

Fuck, this is bad. Bad, bad, bad. Damn it.

Thom scrubbed furiously at the sticky spot on the bar. Or, well, what used to be a sticky spot. After twenty minutes of Thom taking out his frustrations on the bar, all stickiness was long gone and the entire wooden length shone like a mirror.

He didn't care. The fury, the fear and especially the thrice-damned, annoying *desire*, had to be worked out somehow, or he'd end up exploding at a customer. If Phil the Boss was anything like Phil the Insatiable Sex Monster, he'd be reasonable enough to let it go with a warning, but Thom didn't feel like betting his job on that. He still hoped the Rosewood job would come through, but for now he had an income and a temporary home, and he had no intention of risking either just because he was pissed off. Never mind that he had a fucking right to be *royally* pissed off.

Why? Because the two of you hooked up before either of you knew you were working for him? That's not his fault any more than it is yours. Maybe he's just as shaken up by this as you are. You could at least give him a chance.

Thom wrinkled his nose. He hated it when his inner voice guilted away his righteous anger.

He turned to look at the clock behind the bar. Another hour until they opened. Plenty of time to go find Phil and apologize for being a gigantic jackass.

With a put-upon sigh, he hung the rag on a hook behind the bar and stomped across the restaurant toward the kitchen. "I'm going to talk to Phil," he said to Mike, the busboy, who'd been watching him with the wary expression of a mouse trapped behind the sofa by a hungry tabby. "Everything's ready to go. I'll be back in a few minutes."

Mike nodded, brown eyes wide and thin shoulders hunched. Thom shook his head as he stalked across the floor. The kid really needed to grow a pair.

In the kitchen, Circe was writing the lunch specials in bright green marker on a couple of dry erase boards. He nodded in response to her smile, but didn't stop to talk. If he didn't say what he had to say to Phil right now, he'd lose his nerve for sure.

Phil's office door was closed. Thom crossed the storeroom and stood in front of it, heart hammering and knees shaking, and tried to summon the courage to knock. He didn't mind apologizing for being a jerk, and he didn't think for a second that Phil would try anything unethical. Phil wasn't the type of person who would use his position as the boss to extort sex from his employees.

No, Thom's biggest fear was much simpler. If Phil touched him again, or gave him that slow, wicked smile, he wouldn't be able to stop himself from having the man right there in the office. The tip of his finger still burned with the lingering warmth of Phil's kiss.

God, his lips are so fucking soft.

Grimacing, Thom shook off the haze of desire threatening to overpower him. *Get it together, Thom. Just knock on the door, and when he opens it, say you're sorry, shake his hand and go back to work. You can do this.*

He drew a deep breath, blew it out and lifted his hand. Before his knuckles could make contact with the scarred wood, however, the door opened, and Thom found himself face-to-collarbone with Phil.

Thom looked up to meet Phil's gaze. "Um. Hi."

"Hey." Phil gave him a cautious smile. "What's up, Bu...I

mean, Thom?"

"I, uh, I just wanted to say I'm sorry. For how I acted before." Thom wiped his damp palms on his jeans. "So, yeah. Sorry. I was surprised, is all."

Phil's smile widened. "No problem. I was kind of surprised myself."

The mischievous twinkle in Phil's hazel eyes had Thom's head whirling with thoughts completely inappropriate for the workplace. He swallowed, fighting the urge to shove his hand inside those ridiculous black cargo shorts Phil wore and wrap his fingers around the man's impressive prick. "Okay. Well, bye."

Thom turned to go. A big hand clamped onto his arm, stopping him in his tracks. "Where're you going?" Phil voice rumbled behind him, far too close for comfort.

"Back to work." Thom winced at the transparent lust in his voice. "Please let go."

Phil's hand fell away, but the solid warmth of his body pressed to Thom's back, freezing him in place. "You know I won't hold this over you, right?" Phil's breath stirred the hair at Thom's temple when he spoke.

"I know." Thom smiled over his shoulder. "It's just kind of strange working for someone who's had his tongue up your ass, you know?"

A low, needy sound emerged from somewhere deep in Phil's chest. He rested one open palm on Thom's hip. "I want you," he whispered, stray wisps of silky hair brushing Thom's ear. "And I'm not afraid to go after what I want. But I won't ever pressure you. If you want to end it right here, right now, just be friends, I'm cool with that." His head dipped, his lips nuzzling Thom's neck. "You want me, though, you just say the word."

Printed in the United States
148908LV00002B/48/P

9 781605 043197